Books in

The Human-Hybrid Project

series:

The Electrified Sword

The Electrified Sword

Farley L. Dunn

THREE SKILLET

Published in Fort Worth, Texas

 THREE SKILLET

www.ThreeSkilletPublishing.com

Three Skillet Publishing
PO Box 162194
Fort Worth, Texas 76161

ISBN: 978-1-957173-08-5

Printed in the USA

The Electrified Sword

— Book 9 —

The Human-Hybrid Project

Corona Tower Research Complex

Basement Level 1

Underground Parking

Military Housing

Offices

Cafeteria

Tower Footprint and Main Elevator

Storage Tanks

Research Center Main Lobby

Basement Level 2

Staffing Housekeeping

Research Labs

Garik's Quarters

Basement Level 3

Emergency Clinic

Corona City

Cafeteria

Living Space Failed Hybrids

Recreation Area

Natatorium

Soundproof Training Cells

Cages for Animals

Storage

Cafeteria

Power Plant

Hospital

Basement Level 4

Utility Right of Way

Basement Level 5

Key:

1 Block

Corona Tower
Your Home Away from Home

Penthouse Level
40th Floor →

Weston Rodheimer's
Penthouse Suite

Halo Sunchaser's
Apartment

Floor 7 →

Stamford Suites
Grill, Pool
and Gym

Jantzen Hefferly/
Garik Shayk's
Apartment

Floors 2-6 →

Stamford Suites
Hotel and
Apartments

First Floor →

Lobby and
Glass-Walled
Atrium

← **Open to**
the Mall →

Chow Down and
the Elevator Entrance
to the Rest of the
Tower

Cassel Bay

Bay City

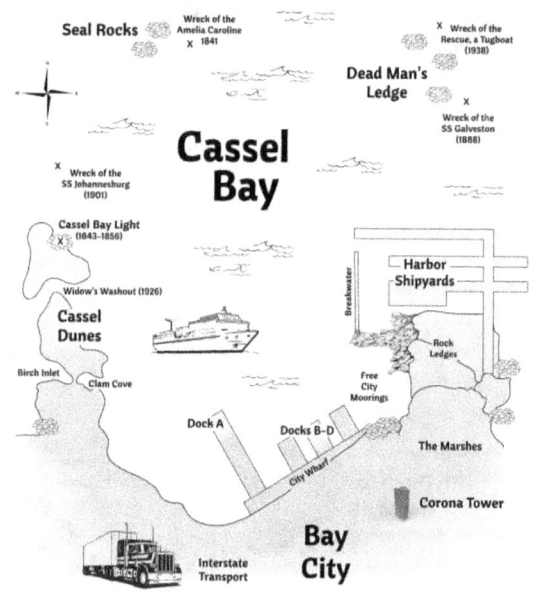

Seal Rocks

Wreck of the
Amelia Caroline
X 1841

X Wreck of the
Rescue, a Tugboat
(1938)

Dead Man's
Ledge

X
Wreck of the
SS Galveston
(1888)

Cassel
Bay

X
Wreck of the
SS Johannesburg
(1901)

Cassel Bay Light
X (1843-1856)

Widow's Washout (1926)

Breakwater

Harbor
Shipyards

Cassel
Dunes

Rock
Ledges

Birch Inlet

Clam Cove

Free
City
Moorings

Dock A

Docks B-D

The Marshes

City Wharf

Corona Tower

Interstate
Transport

Bay
City

— I —

H

alo Sunchaser towered over Garik Shayk, and the light of her electrified sword cast fractured shadows around the bronze-skinned teen, creating brittle shards of darkness that reached out to slice anyone who dared draw too close. The rest of Corona Tower's underground parking garage was dark, the lights shattered by the sword as its power had arced through the air to consume Jantzen Hefferly, Garik's mentor and the man he had come to think of as a father figure.

In her black-and-red kaftan, with her ebony skin, Sunchaser looked a vengeful goddess. Pools of spilled ink danced as she exulted in her victory. Second-in-command in the secretive human-hybrid research project and modified with the DNA of a hawk, she had the avian's intense stare and saw herself as homo superior, a class above ordinary people.

Jantzen Hefferly, hybridized with squid DNA and able to sublimate directly from a solid to a purple mist and the second subject to be hybridized in Corona Tower's secretive human-hybrid project, had proved a threat to Sunchaser, and now he was gone.

Garik was also modified, but not by choice. He had been forcibly inducted into the Tower's highly classified human-hybrid program in an effort to create the military's perfect super soldier, but his gene-enhanced quickness from his timber wolf DNA hadn't been enough to save his mentor.

"Halo," a voice roared. "Brace's men are arriving." Weston Rodheimer, the Director of the underground research facility, with his gorilla-like shoulders and rumbling voice, intervened to take control of the situation. With each word, his limbs erupted in sparks of white-hot electricity, a fireworks display to compete with the electrified sword. Colonel Brace had vied with Rodheimer for control of the Tower's super soldier project. He had disbursed his paramilitary team of hybrid soldiers—magnificently powerful but fatally flawed—

to step in when rioting had threatened the stability of Bay City and the Tower's military-funded human-hybrid project.

"I am rid of Jantzen. Let them come!" Sunchaser vibrated with her success. The electrified sword flashed in the darkened parking garage, a brilliant beacon casting harsh, otherworldly shadows, the symbol of Sunchaser's fiery triumph over Jantzen in her bid to cement her position in Corona Tower's power structure.

"Halo," Rodheimer stepped close to her, the sparks from his skin fainter only in comparison to the blazing sword, "I will break you if you reveal a working sword to Brace."

"I just won, and people are cheering me, *me*, Weston, not Jantzen. I can take anyone who comes against us."

"Not without me, and I don't intend to play."

"I don't need your permission. The sword is my creation—"

"And it took you how long to charge, twelve hours, fifteen? There will be fifty men here in minutes. Think again before you consider this your best option. We mustn't give away everything we can do."

Garik's attention jerked from his immersion in Jantzen's horrific death to Sunchaser and Rodheimer. *Don't give away everything you can do.* Those had been some of the first words Jantzen had said to him. He watched Sunchaser deflate in the face of the truth. The light from the sword was fading in intensity, telling the reality of her ability to wield it against multiple enemies.

The night had been cold, and with the growing shadows filling the parking facility, people began moving toward the doors of the underground research center for light and warmth. The back wall of the massive parking garage, now bathed in darkness, fronted Lowell Street and provided a secretive back entrance for military access to the outside world. Tires hit the concrete, ripping rubber, as the Lowell Street entrance erupted with five military transports.

Rodheimer turned his attention to Garik. "Get up from there, boy. Where is your chaperone?"

"There." Garik pointed. Devon Maye, the research center's activities director, now confined to a manual wheelchair, sat with one leg propped on a leg extension. Garik had escaped the facility twice. His movements up and down Corona Tower were now tightly controlled, and Devon Maye was his jailer. He was being reined in once more.

"Go. Is that clear?" Rodheimer radiated fury.

"Yes," Garik assented, even as he fought what he wanted to say. *No, Director. Things aren't the least clear. Sunchaser has just killed my friend and mentor. How is that going to be dealt with?* Yet, he didn't want the Director's fury focused on him or on the activities director. That part *was* perfectly clear. Anger at

Sunchaser swirled in him, bleeding from him until every object around him vibrated with a rainbow sheen of churning color. He whispered his mantra, "My hands, my mind, my desire," to keep the rainbows at bay.

"Now," the Director growled.

Garik felt his control slip. The parking garage bled color, the rainbows surging in a pyroclastic eruption from every crack, and the world slowed around him until he was a blur, a ghost, a whisper in the darkness. A rainbow god who could move at the speed of light. Seemingly without moving, he was beside Devon, the rainbows evaporated into wisps of color, and Garik was once more a youth who should be finishing his senior year at Bay City High.

Except that final year in high school had been stolen when he was inducted forcibly into the Tower's human-hybrid project, and now that he was in, he could never be out.

THE MILITARY vehicles swung around, stopped hard, the doors opened, and paramilitary hybrid soldiers fell out and to attention, wrapped in black with a stylized white eagle flying on each arm and heads encased in helmets with hockey puck-shaped breathing apparatuses for mouthpieces. Colonel William Brace exited more sedately, with the false genial charm of a would-be Southern gentleman. A solid man with a firm way of placing each step, his straight back and white hair made him a visual force to be reckoned with.

Garik wondered if the four hybrid soldiers he had defeated in Brace's rigged contest were among them, Luis Rodrigo, Samuel Jameson, Huey Hyatt, and Wally Simpson. Their cheat weapons—sanctioned by Colonel Brace—had been a wrist-mounted stun-stud carried by Rodrigo, a full stun gun from Jameson, a steel knife from Hyatt's sleeve, and an electroknife from inside the collar of Simpson's boot. With the helmets, he likely wouldn't be able to tell. The paramilitary troops were identically hybridized, so they displayed a uniform build and height. Their faces or their manner of walking sometimes gave them away, but Garik hunched his shoulders in an effort to be inconspicuous.

Rodheimer called to Brace, "Colonel, what can we do for you?"

"Tell me what's going on in my building." The man held out a hand to tell his men to hold back, and he walked Rodheimer's direction as he spoke.

"Your building?" The Director looked at Sunchaser, took in her expression, and turned to the colonel. "I assume you mean the building you have temporarily and illegally commandeered by sheer force."

"If you must, but mine, nonetheless." The colonel seemed pleased with Rodheimer's admission of his command.

"I wouldn't know, Colonel. This is Corona Tower,

home for my research center. Bay City High is three blocks east. If you follow Stamford south to Corona and go east, you will eventually reach the school." He turned with Sunchaser and began to walk away.

By this time, most people had returned to the building. Several dozen Airmen were busy at their equipment, either working on it or pretending to while they listened to what could become a very entertaining headbutt session. A few others were scattered here and there, several of them hybrid. They wanted to be part of the entertainment, also. They weren't usually permitted into the garage, but they hadn't been stopped during the melee with Jantzen Hefferly and his clash with the electrified sword.

It surprised Garik that many of the hybrid program participants had no interest in escaping. Governments from across the world sent their brightest and best to the Tower for a chance to be part of the super soldier human-hybrid program. If it worked, they were one step closer to creating a whole new level of military power. If not, then the secrecy of the program kept the world from being the wiser.

Garik hadn't been chosen by his government. He hadn't volunteered. And each time he'd tried to escape, he had been pursued, hounded, and BolaWrapped . . . nearly killed to get him back. He looked to the ramp leading upwards into the open air and to Bay City. He could do it, run. Leap so fast the world became a rainbow-hued blur and be out that door before anyone in this place knew he was gone. He could. *He could!* And still, the facts didn't change. He no longer lived in that world. He had been hybridized with timber wolf DNA and now boasted eight extra inches in height, a heart and lung capacity that gave him impossible durability, a newly flexible spine and elasticized tendons that amped up his speed blurringly fast, and ears that could hear a pin drop in the next room.

And then came the mental changes: increased memory, smell recognition, and what came very close to precognition, except Garik's was more like listen, evaluate, and extrapolate. He was rarely wrong.

"Hey, kiddo, think we should go in? This is over with." Devon socked his arm with a fist. He sounded like he wanted it to be over with.

And that was another thing Garik had gotten from his timber wolf DNA, the instinct to protect the pack. His pack outside of the Tower had been stolen from him, his girlfriend killed, his aunt alienated by her scummy boyfriend, his parents in far-off Russia. Every person he could share what had been done to him was here—in the Tower or escaped from it—and he didn't know if they lived or died, except Justin Kurtew, who was hybridized with a praying mantis—giving both awesome and horrifying results—and Alyna Lindberg, hybridized with a Komodo dragon, giving her massive claws that she could extend at will. They had come to rescue Jantzen and had gotten him this far before Sunchaser had chewed him up with her electrified sword.

The three escaped hybrids who had been captured with Jantzen were likely still in the research center's hospital on Basement 4, but Garik didn't know for sure. After surviving the artificial lightning-induced sonic boom that had created a pressure wave so strong that it had prevented Jantzen from sublimating from his solid form directly to a gaseous purple mist, their injuries had to be severe. Hybrids were sturdy and healed quickly, but the blast had shattered windows and pulverized concrete. Paolo Leveen, Giselle Harmon, Julia Cantos, all lost as far as Garik knew.

Who was Garik's pack? Right now it was Devon Maye. A wolf doesn't abandon the pack, not in peacetime, and especially not in a time of crisis.

"Okay, Devo, I agree. Let's head in."

However, several of the black goons with the white eagles on their sleeves had come close enough to recognize an old opponent.

"Hey, there's the thief." One goon pulled off his helmet, which was perfectly safe while he was in low-activity mode. It was when he hiked his metabolism to battle readiness that his body would not be able to metabolize the required oxygen from the air. The oxygen concentrator in its hockey puck shape did that for him. With his helmet gone, he revealed wiry blond hair and a scar running down his face. "Did you enjoy my stunner, scum? You had no right to it. My property, and I want it back."

"Jameson," Brace called, his voice loud and sharp. When the blond man didn't respond, Brace turned to another man. "Rodrigo, control your man or you *will* be in the kitchen tonight peeling potatoes."

"Private Jameson!" The man, Rodrigo, still helmeted, lifted a stone from the floor, let it fly surprisingly hard, and impacted Jameson in the back of the head.

"Hey, I ain't no private." Jameson rubbed his head.

"You will be if you continue down the road you're on. Helmet on, mister. We are here to do a job, not play out your private fantasies."

"You and your crip friend, I don't forget a face." Jameson shoved his helmet on his head, and he turned to walk away, his tree trunk legs pumping in his black suit.

"Hey, kiddo, I can walk if you don't want to push." Devon's voice was barely under control.

"I could take him," Garik growled as he set the wheelchair into motion.

"And I'm in a cast. I couldn't."

And you're my pack. I'd do it for you. He didn't say that. It was understood. It's just the way wolves were.

Timber wolves, especially, and that was Garik, bone and marrow. Human was what he used to be. Now, he was more.

— 2 —

A

s Garik and Devon moved back into the research center, the mood had already taken a celebratory air, especially among the hybrids. The main campus cafeteria, where most of the successful hybrids were required to dine, was on the lobby level—Basement Level 1—and as Garik and Devon walked by, a jubilant cheerfulness spilled out.

"So, my friend is killed, and they celebrate." Garik growled the words under his breath.

"You're just behind me, kiddo. I can hear you." Devon's voice was calmer but barely steady. "Jantzen's not the issue. The sword is. Let's go in, catch the tone of the crowd. Besides, I haven't seen some of these people since Kevin stepped in to help me out."

Devon would know most of them. As the activities director—and he would be again as soon as his cast was removed—he had planned and overseen most of their training regimens and could call them by name.

A familiar group was off to one side, already in party mode, and Garik headed Devon's wheelchair their direction.

"Devon!" A coffee-colored woman with a dark halo of hair called to them. Melanie Hatherill was modified for speed but with DNA from a hippopotamus. Instead of Garik's tall, lithe shape, with his flexible backbone, she wore long legs and a high waist, a different enhancement for quickness. She spoke in a separated, hard fashion, each word coming across as a complete sentence. "Come. We. Are. Having. A. Discussion."

"Cripple!" Louise King, wearing a flowing robe to disguise the winglike structures under her arms, her nod to her butterfly extraction. She displayed bright and colorful designs undulating across her pale skin. She could retain and release toxins at a touch, a deadly tactic if she wished to deploy it.

"Not much longer, Louise," Devon responded. "I can already walk if my slave will get my crutches."

"Yes, massa." Garik picked up on what Devon had just done: diluted the reason they were together. No one would ask why Garik was with Devon, forcing them to explain that the younger man was under constant supervision by chaperones to keep him from Houdini-ing from the Tower once again. It would appear he was there to help Devon navigate the vast research center, and they would accept him as such. So, he retrieved the crutches from across the room and leaned them against the table.

"Hey, man, you're keeping this loser from stagnating in his own self-pity. Appreciate you." Joachim Warakaulle, modified with a lobster, wore a self-imposed South Pacific vibe, with skin color and hair to match. He had received special enzymes that modified and repaired his DNA when in high need situations. "*They* want us to lose focus, shatter without them constantly over us. The overlords think we peons can't exist without their guiding light. Man, they don't know us at all. But you, Garik, my man, what's with the new tallness? Thought you were all wolf, not part giraffe." He smiled and shot him a thumbs up.

"The better to eat you with, my dear." Garik's words came out sharper than he intended, as Joachim had done nothing to incite his irritation, but Sunchaser sure had, and he felt it seething just under his skin.

"The wolf now has a bite." Mike Lamonte, bovine-enhanced, with tousled hair and large eyes. "I smell anger. Is that anger I smell, anyone, anyone?"

"Was no one besides me out there?" Garik looked hard at them, Melanie, Louise, Joachim, Mike, and several others. He mocked Mike's repeated word. "Anyone, anyone? Did you see what happened? Jantzen just killed? Or am I the only one that noticed?"

"Sweetie, we noticed." Charlotte Mnich, covered by bright iridescent patches from her hummingbird DNA, tried to soothe him.

"Sweetie, we noticed," came from behind Garik in Charlotte's exact tone and modulation.

"Anatoli or Andrey?" Garik didn't need to turn to know it was one of the Burgorski twins. The tall, full-featured men had dark hair and pale skin. Their skill at mimicry came from their mockingbird DNA. Anatoli could be distinguished by a break in his right eyebrow from a childhood injury, and Andrey boasted a small mole by his left eye. Garik turned to find both men now shorter than him.

"We've shrunk." Anatoli laughed, touching his brother on the arm.

"No, Anati, I think not." Andrey looked thoughtful. "You may have shrunk. I am the same size. Garik is now a mountain."

"A mountain." Anatoli laughed again. "I know a mountain man. That's a first."

"Are you idiots done?" Garik was about to punch some faces in. Jantzen was dead. Did no one care?

"No," Anatoli said, grinning, "but what did you need?" He looked around the group to gauge their reactions.

"You people are on a completely different wavelength from me." Garik saw Fabiola Bello standing at the back of the group, a thick-bodied girl with a muscular stance and spiky blonde hair. It had been a while since he'd spoken with her, but he hadn't forgotten her honeybee-infused ability to read a situation. "Fabi, what am I missing?"

And he *was* missing something. His anger, perhaps, was throwing him off. Normally, he was outstanding at reading a situation, evaluating the information, and extrapolating what was coming. Now, he seemed a sheep in wolf's clothing. A beast on the outside and really stupid where it counted.

Fabiola pulled a chair free, whipped her leg over it, and was seated, the picture of agility. She narrowed her eyes at Garik and reminded him, "You left me stranded in an elevator once."

"Sorry about that." She and her group had been mocking Devon unmercifully, and he had taken her passkey from the elevator and inserted Raphaël Giannotti's.

"And took my passkey."

"You got it back, didn't you?" Sheesh, this wasn't about passkeys. A man had been *killed*.

Raphaël, to the side, with tree-trunk legs and a gray

cast to his skin, opened his eyes wide, produced a pass-key from a pocket, and held it out for everyone to see.

Fabiola took it, said, "Replaced it with Raphaël's. Best trick, ever," and she grinned. "Can you teach me that?"

"It's part of my DNA." The wolf part. "It's not something you can learn. Are you going to help me, or should I just go it alone *again*?"

"Notches, notches," Andrey said, sounding very much like Devon.

"I do say that," Devon admitted, chuckling.

"And you also say to take it down one." Anatoli this time. "But I'm enjoying this. Fabi, tell the man what he's missing, cause I'm missing it, too."

"We all," and she looked around at the others with her, "like Jantzen. Well, liked, after what happened today."

"Yeah."

"He was the best."

"Loved his magic show. Looked like real magic."

"Stood up for us."

"Okay," Fabiola said. "Enough eulogies. See, Jantzen's been gone a long time. When he left, we understood why, but he's made it hard for all of us."

"Lockdowns." Mike, the word harsh.

"And this whole military thing. Brace was looking for an opportunity, and Jantzen handed it to him." Joachim. "Never give the man the power. Always keep it in reserve, that's what I say. It's the class struggle. Jantz let us down on that."

"He was saving those people." Garik had to defend him. And the military thing? That was on him. He was taken aback that they didn't realize it was all about Rodheimer and Brace feuding over him. "They were being sent to Level 5. You know what happens on Level 5."

"Sweetie, that's why it's hard." Charlotte, with her iridescent hummingbird skin. "We loved them, respected them, wanted the best for them. But we all know when we sign up for this what the rules are. Jantzen did what he thought best for them, but it wasn't best for us."

"Jantzen needed to be taken down a notch, even if I think using the sword was too much. That was a harsh way to meet your end." Raphaël shook his head.

"But the sword!" Joachim's eyes glowed with excitement. "To see it like that, in the open, the power! Man, we could make the class struggle a thing of the past with that."

Garik was filled with despair trying to make them understand. Jantzen was dead. Nothing outweighed that.

LIVING AT the top of the forty-story Corona tower in Jantzen's old apartment, and monitored with each outing he took, Garik's thumb on the pulse of the basement research campus was filtered by several screens. Devon, occasionally, though he was mostly with him when no one else was available. He had seen Kevin Lee, the man who was acting as Devon's interim activities director, only a few times, and as he didn't live in the Tower, he sometimes knew less than Garik. The rest of his minders had no connection with the research center and likely didn't know it existed. They were highly efficient but clueless cogs in a giant machine that was there for the sole purpose of hiding the super soldier production facility in the building's enormous five-story basement complex.

Garik admitted he had seen much of what Fabiola and the others had described in his own relationship with Jantzen. He could be manipulative and secretive, and at times, Garik had wanted more from the man than he seemed inclined to give, even stepping away occasionally when Garik had needed him most. Still, when a man you've come to think of as a father figure makes a misstep, it doesn't sever your attachment to him. You forgive and move on. Your relationship is built on the good things between you, and there were plenty of those with Jantzen.

Man, he missed the guy, to use Joachim's expression.

Garik's first real clue that something big was happening came two weeks in while meeting Kevin for an early-morning visit to the climbing wall.

"Okay, my friend. Devon has suggested some climbing wall challenges for you." It was breakfast, and they were in the Stamford Suites Grill. Ted Charles, the manager, had been excited to see them and had welcomed them with fresh croissants steaming in a basket.

"I'm more awake at ten." Garik was awake enough, however, to break open one of the croissants and inhale the steam before biting into it.

"Ten's not good. Seven is."

"I can see." The clock on the wall showed a quarter of. "Who are you seeing at ten?" Kevin was the acting activities director through the end of the week. Devon would be taking over again then.

"No one." Kevin chewed and swallowed a bit of bread, then dripped honey on a fresh roll. "The ceremony. I'm surprised you haven't heard. Everyone will be there."

"Stop the guessing game. What haven't I heard?"

"Ms. Sunchaser is getting a promotion. The lobby will be filled."

"The lobby will be filled." Garik searched his head. Lobby . . . promotion . . . he couldn't put it together.

"Still doing that, huh? How do they say it? You can take the boy out of the country, but you can't take the country out of the boy. Isn't that it?"

"I've never lived in the country. Well, since being here. Back in Russia—"

"See? Can't take the country out of the boy, and

you keep repeating what other people say, not that I mind. It reminds me that you're still the little Garik I first invited to Ai Kee! inside that huge body you have now."

"But what's special about Ms. Sunchaser's promotion that the entire research center is attending?"

Kevin hesitated, and he groaned and bumped his forehead with his knuckles. "Ouch. I shouldn't have mentioned it. I didn't even think. There's a reason they kept you in the dark. You likely don't want to know."

"I do want to know."

"Probably not. I shouldn't tell you anything else, not if I value my job—"

"Kevin—" Garik growled the word, and it came out a wolf-like snarl.

"Hey, wolf boy, don't gnaw my leg. I'm just the messenger. It's a reward for the, um, incident in the underground garage."

"The incident." Where she had killed Jantzen with the electrified sword.

"See, that wasn't so bad, and I have my little Garik back."

No, Kevin didn't have his "little Garik" back. To celebrate Sunchaser? For killing the man he looked up to as his father?

The idea was impossible to contain.

— 3 —

G

arik's fist flew into the punching bag, sending a cloud of talcum powder flying in the impact. His hand wrap vibrated with the force of the hit. It was nearly ten, and he knew what was happening at ten.

"So, Jantzen is killed, and they give her a promotion." Garik growled the words, and he slammed into the punching bag again.

"Easy, champ," Kofi Mandela called. He was officially the Stamford Suites pool boy, but he also served as gofer and general "fill in the blank" positions. Right now, he was assigned to oversee Garik's time in the Stamford Suites gym for training.

"Easy, champ," Garik repeated as he slammed one fist for each word into the punching bag, his anger a storm cloud that threatened to break at any time.

"Come on, Garik, you can damage the bag. And you're seriously punching it. We don't have a spare."

Garik turned his head to take in Kofi sitting on the corner of a table, one leg hanging and the other on the floor, in his standard Corona Tower polo and shorts with canvas shoes. His tight hair was freshly trimmed in a braided look. He emanated an aroma of sun and water.

"Do you have any real clothes?" Garik wiped his forehead with the back of one arm. "Like these types of clothes?" He punched the bag hard, sending a haze of talcum into the air.

"And do you have to use talcum powder at the punching bag? That's what I want to know." Kofi held a tablet, and he hadn't looked up yet.

"What do you care?" Garik faced the bag and punched it twice more, wham! wham! and looked back to Kofi. "You've yet to join me in a practice session once. You know that? Every day you're with me, and not once have you joined in."

"Not my job." Kofi finally looked up. Kofi had been taller than Garik when they first met, but in the past months, Garik had outstripped him. Kofi was no wimp, however.

"Let's make it your job. How about that?" Wham, wham!

"Like in the pool? Once was enough for me." On their first training session, Kofi had pushed Garik hard. As a reward, Garik had tossed Kofi in the pool. Kofi hadn't let him forget.

"Not enough for me." Garik punched again and again, faster and faster, not letting up, blanking out everything except the blurring of his fists into the bag.

"Enough," Kofi said, this time at Garik's back, and he touched his shoulder to get his attention.

The connection of hand to skin whirled Garik around, and in a blur of gym and punching bag and treadmills and braided hair and sun and water and Corona colors, Kofi was flat of his back, and Garik knelt over him, his forearm against the man's chest, leaving Kofi's eyes wide with a look of . . . amazement? fear? shock?

"Not enough," Garik said, not even winded. "Not enough, ever, Kofi. C'mon, get changed and challenge me. Show me you're better than me. I'm up for it."

"I don't know if I am. You don't see how fast you move. Off."

Kofi made to push Garik aside, but Garik held against him, not giving, until he saw the man's eyes harden in frustration. Then Garik was up, quick, in one motion, leaving Kofi still flat on the floor.

"You need help?" Garik cocked his head and raised an eyebrow.

"Would you give it?" Kofi went up on his elbows.

"Only if you needed it."

Kofi held out a hand, and Garik effortlessly pulled him to his feet. The pool boy leaned down to retrieve his tablet, checked it to be sure it was still working, and shook his head.

"Did I worry you?" Garik rested a hand on the punching bag, setting it swaying the smallest amount.

"You're too good to worry me. Surprised me, yes, but you have too much control to make me think you don't know exactly what you intend. What's got you so angry?"

Garik wanted to answer. To share. Have someone know his frustration, drain the wound, tell him that Sunchaser had been wrong, wrong, wrong to do what she did. But Kofi was a Tower employee, not privy to the secrets of the classified research center in the Tower's basement. And while Kofi wasn't part of Garik's core pack, not the one he had truly bonded with, he was on the perimeter. Garik felt a measure of protectiveness toward the man. They spent time together nearly every day working in training sessions around the man's real work schedule supervising the pool for Stamford Suites guests, and he had no desire to jeopardize his job with the Director.

Protect the pack. Above all else, protect the pack.

THE AFTERNOON brought a return of Kevin Lee.

"How was the shindig?" Garik sat on a bench in the basement changing rooms, readying for a session doing real boxing, not the nonsense where he pounded a bag and someone sat on the side watching, meaning *watching Garik when he wasn't watching his tablet.*

"I told you this morning that you don't want to know." Kevin was wrapping one of Garik's hands. He would wear gloves this time as he would have a real opponent, and hand wraps in the gloves made it easier on his hands—or so Kevin said.

Garik suspected he wouldn't notice the difference. When he started hitting, his anger dam burst, and he didn't feel his hands. And he healed really quick, so what did it matter?

"Here's what I need you to think about." Kevin worked a glove over one wrapped hand and began tying the laces. "Kofi told me about you and the punching bag this morning—"

"Stupid Kofi." Garik narrowed his eyes and looked away.

"Don't give me that. Kofi's a good guy, and he enjoys working with you. Be nice to him." Kevin patted the first glove, and he tapped Garik's other hand with a balled fist for him to hold it out.

"He's afraid I'll damage the equipment. And maybe

I would, but when I start, the anger comes out, and—"

"You have good reason to be angry. Don't let the anger control you."

"Too late for that." The rainbows. They did control him if he wasn't careful, causing him to slip into a frenzy state that he couldn't easily cut off. He could see the connection, just not how to resolve it.

"It's never too late. Hold your arm steady." He had the second hand wrapped, placed the glove over it and shoved hard, forcing it over the hand, then pulled Garik's gloved hand against his stomach and began to lace it.

"Why no talcum?" Garik always did, felt it kept his wraps and gloves fresher.

"I use a dryer when you're finished. No need for talcum. Don't be a wimp. This is the best way. Hold out both your hands." Kevin lined them up, looked at them critically as if one might be different from the other, and satisfied, he clapped them on the outside, knocking them together, and said, "Good to go. You're sparring with Samey Borat today."

"Big guy, hairy?"

"Same Samey."

"He's what, grizzly?" The man was built like one.

"Kodiak, if my sources are correct. I asked Devon to sit in. He loses his cast this week. Don't expect him to be a hundred percent right away, but he really wants back in play."

"We're losing you, then." Garik stood, smashed the gloves together, and shook his arms.

"Like you could arrange that." Kevin laughed. "Buddy, you've got to beat me harder than that to chase me off. Did you miss the 'don't expect him to be a hundred percent' part? I'll be around for a while."

"Good."

"Oh, and why is that?" Kevin was packing things up, and he had his attention on his equipment bag.

"I need someone in my corner."

"Like I said, Devon's coming this afternoon."

"You know what I mean." Garik smashed his gloves together again, frustrated that the man didn't seem to understand.

"No, what do you mean?" Kevin, still in the bag, taking a long time sorting out the equipment.

"You're important to me." Garik's stomach turned at the admission. He had said it, and now it was out there. It frightened him that it could come back and bite him.

"What?" Kevin looked up. "I didn't catch that."

"I said—" irritation caused Garik to growl the words, "you're important to me."

"Yah! I thought that's what I heard!" Kevin leaped to his feet, smashed a fist into Garik's shoulder, and laughed. "Took me long enough to pull it from you. Let's go smash some face. Just not *too* much smash!" He hefted the equipment bag to the bench, grabbed a set of towels, and was out the door.

Garik stared at the closing door, feeling silly. That was something he didn't have figured out. As he moved toward the exit, he caught himself in the mirror. His height, but he had grown used to that. His hair, long enough to actively curl but not long enough to be tempered by length. His eyes, gray with gold flecks and just a hint of eyeshine under the changing room lights. His Armenian features and bronze skin, the most familiar thing about him.

What caught his attention was his shoulders, the definition in his arms, his waist, the way his shorts hung on his hips. Someone he didn't know. A man, not a boy. Someone formed from human and timber wolf DNA to be a super soldier, different than he had been—better, bigger, stronger.

He was bigger. And stronger, too. Better? A super soldier? He didn't see it, yet. He was still Garik, perhaps not quite human, but still wanting to be.

No rainbows today, Garik, he chided himself. *You don't need the rainbows. You're good enough on your own.* He tightened his arm, watched the muscles flex, and felt good.

Yet, as he exited the room, he doubted his own words. He was the rainbows. They were the new Garik, and until he learned to control them, they were more Garik than he was.

SAMEY BORAT took no second-place trophies when he stood in the ring. Bear country faced Garik, and it looked like Samey Borat. The man was every bit the bear's DNA he hailed from. Paws, claws, fur, and torso. Limbs of seasoned oak. Human in shape but clearly extra. Like the strongman at the circus that can lift the elephant, and you wonder if he's wearing a padded suit until the elephant's feet are six inches in the air.

"Garik," Samey called in greeting. He lifted his snout, er, his chin and huffed twice after saying Garik's name. He also had boxing gloves on, but they were twice Garik's size. He crunched them together, and the man's arms flexed with power.

"Samey," Garik returned, unsure that he was the equal of this man. Brace's goons? He *knew* he could take them, and they were big. Samey? The pit in Garik's stomach suggested fear.

He scanned the observers for Devon—there were a surprising number present—and found him standing beside Annie Vanschooneveld. He was propped up with his crutches but had one arm entwined with hers. He nodded, and Devon returned the motion. It seemed the hybrid crowd was making an afternoon of it. Steven Klandermans, Ineke Van Stekelenburg, Jacquelien Van Kessel, Bert Ellis, Lansana Opoku-Mensah, Veronika Abbink, Zekeria Salem. He noted the absence of Paul, but then Paul had been face down in the parking garage the last time he'd seen him, and that told the story of that.

Benjamin Fuest? Garik would have been surprised to see him. He barely had motive to say hello, much less gather to see the show.

Zekeria Salem was off by himself, separate from Raphaël, Fabiola, or any of the others that Garik and Devon had visited with the day of Sunchaser's betrayal.

It was when Weston Rodheimer and a newly glowing Halo Sunchaser entered the viewing area that something shifted inside Garik. In his mind, she held the sword aloft, and the white electricity of its energy blast reached out for Jantzen and absorbed him molecule by molecule, atom by atom, until there was nothing left. Fury rose up in him, filling every limb, every digit, every part of who he was. His skin could not hold it in, and the rainbows filled the room, swirling until there was nothing else.

He let out a snarl, filled with understanding. *Anger.* Emotion strong enough to override his control was key. This time, the fury of what Sunchaser had done served as his trigger. In his rage, nothing else mattered except the rainbows.

Let the frenzy begin!

— 4 —

G

arik swam upward through the murky haze. At the top was air and light and . . . and not the boxing ring.

"I've done it again, and I don't know what I've done." Garik moaned and fell back into the haze. He let himself be swallowed up, unwilling to deal with the ramifications of whatever *thing* he had messed up *again*.

"A NEW family is moving in." Irina, Garik's aunt, was

just in from work at Fasst Market, and she set several bags on the counter with *Fasst Market* emblazoned across the front. They would be from the reduced aisle but still good, if they were consumed before too long. The breads would keep a few extra days on the top shelf of the fridge.

"That's nice." Garik, a small eleven, and slender, with the bush of brown hair and the gray eyes he knew so well, was on the couch. The coffee table was covered with a radio he'd discovered beside the dumpster, and he was certain he could repair it.

"You could help them carry boxes. They have a girl about your age."

"Why do I care about that?" He visibly shivered. He was more interested in skateboards and gaming and two-wheel, go-fast machines, even if he didn't have any of those.

"She's pretty. Her parents own The Flower Shop on Sycamore. You know the place. They put out flowers by the door every day even in cold weather."

He shrugged, intent on his radio. Doing stuff like repairing things made sense to him, and he liked it when they began to work again.

"And they might give you a dollar if you help them."

"Five dollars," he whispered, focused on a broken connector. He looked at it, considering if it could be fixed. Maybe he could trade his time for someone's help.

"They might give you five dollars."

"A box."

"Maybe not, Gari. Be reasonable." Irina walked to him, took the broken part from his hand, looked at it, and handed it back. "Maybe enough to repair this."

"Okay, I'll go." He wiped his hands and stood.

"I knew you would. You're a good boy, Gari. I'm glad you came to live with me." She tousled his hair and pushed him away. "Off with you before they get finished."

At the door, he stopped and asked, "What's her name?"

"Marisa, I think her mother said. She has an older sister, Marina. Or maybe I have it backwards. You can ask."

"I will. Bye, Iri."

And that was the day he met Marisa.

THIS TIME Garik came a little closer to the surface. He looked for the light in the ceiling, the machines along the wall, even the door with the wire-filled safety glass.

"No, Nurse Ratchett," he mumbled. "I'm being good. I don't need more sleepy juice."

He waited for the prick in his arm, and he waited, and he waited, and eventually the room grew darker, until the light faded completely away.

"I WOULD want a jet-assist bike. Maybe a Street Strider."

It was seventh grade, and they were at lunch sitting across from each other. Marisa had a tray lunch with pizza, tater tots, and applesauce. Garik carried a sandwich in a paper bag. His aunt had gone from Fasst Market to Kerre's Dive. She waited tables now, but with bus fare to get there, the money wasn't better.

And there was no "reduced aisle" to soften their grocery bill. Garik carried a paper bag a lot.

"Not me," Marisa said. "I want to be the captain of a ship."

"Seriously?" Garik was skeptical. "Even the lottery wouldn't buy a ship."

"Not own, Gari. That's silly." She laughed and was beautiful. "I want to tell everyone where to sail and how to get there."

"Oh, a people ship."

"They're all people ships. Mine would have guns on the sides in case pirates tried to attack—"

"Pirates!" He shook his head in disbelief. "That's only in movies."

"Do you ever do anything besides fix stuff?" She leaned forward. "I saw a program that said real pirates still attack ships, and they sometimes fight them off with water cannons."

"Okay, then I want to run your water cannons when

you get to be a captain."

"Sure, but first—"

About that time, the bell rang, and they began to gather up their things. Garik never did learn what he had to do to be Marisa's water cannon operator, because the next time they pretended they won the lottery, she had moved on to another dream, one that was bigger and further away than ever before.

GARIK FINALLY reached the surface to a bacon-shrouded mist of delectable aromas. He inhaled, felt good, and opened his eyes to a familiar room, but one that was not his.

"Devon?" He threw back the covers, recognized the pajamas, even if they were small on him. The room was Devon's office. He had stayed here when he lived with him for a time. The bed was familiar, as though Devon had found it useful and never bothered to have it removed. The door was slightly open, and he stepped to it and pulled it wide.

"Good morning, Garik."

"Hello, Annie." Garik felt his face warm. She was in a sleeveless tee and shorts, as if she hadn't yet gotten dressed. She was cooking, and she opened the oven and pulled out a tray of biscuits. Bacon sizzled on the stove.

"Um, where's Devon?" He hung back in the door-way, using it to hide. With his too small pajamas, he felt awkwardly uncomfortable.

"I told Devon those pajamas didn't seem your size, but he assured me you had worn them before." She glanced at him and smiled. "I've set you out some clothes in Devon's bathroom. You go change, and I'll finish this up."

"Okay, thanks." He scooted past her, feeling like a small boy, and dashed for the bathroom. Inside, he closed the door and looked in the mirror, surprised at himself. An unexpectedly thick coating of hair on his jaw and chin, and his eyes. He turned off the light. Then back on and off again. Full eyeshine, and turning the light off hardly made a difference. That was the murky haze he'd navigated. He'd opened his eyes to a dark room, only it wasn't dark to him. He ran a hand through his hair, felt a difference. An inner and outer coat, with a soft underlayer and stiffer guard hairs. He turned, relieved to see it wasn't growing down the center of his back. And his hands, the aroma of his hair. Musky, canine-like. He sniffed his arm, then his armpit. Not . . . terrible, just not Garik.

Well, not Garik before the fight he didn't remember, but certainly Garik now.

He searched for Devon's razor, found shaving gel under the sink, and set it out. With his face clean, he would feel more like himself. With a shower, he was certain he would smell more like himself . . . or at least like the Garik he used to be.

Timber wolf . . . at least he wasn't something

swampily aquatic. People liked dogs. There were other things that were much worse.

"CAN I ASK some questions?" Garik was at the table, now appropriately dressed in a black turtleneck—a nice nod to Jantzen, thank you, Annie—and gray slacks with leather tassel loafers. He had needed a belt, as his waist was too small for his hips and legs, and he had rummaged through Devon's closet to find one. He'd been surprised to find women's clothes alongside the men's.

"Certainly. Give me a moment." She had put on a thin sweater over pants but wore sandals without socks. She poured two glasses of juice and set them on the table. "Come help yourself."

"Sure." His face warmed again that he'd expected her to hand him his food. It was something Irina would do, and he remembered his dream of her. That was so long ago that he thought he'd forgotten it. He stood, took a plate, and loaded it with food. After he was seated, she gave herself about half the amount and joined him.

"My apologies for the lightweight clothes earlier. We weren't sure when you would wake. I told Devon this afternoon, but as you see, I was wrong." She wasn't contrite, just explaining. "Your questions?"

"That's one of them but not my first. You, here. How?"

"I should have expected that." She laughed lightly

and took a sip of her juice. "Devon wasn't really mobile, so I offered to help. I stayed overnight. Next?"

"Where is Devon? Breakfast—" He motioned to the things on the table. "—he should be here. He's not working, is he? His cast . . . he has . . . had days before it was coming off."

"It's coming off a bit early. I stayed behind in case you woke. So, I get to enjoy breakfast with a handsome young man, and you get breakfast." She smiled. "Any more questions?"

"How bad was the damage if I can't remember anything?" The rainbows . . . how far under did he dive? And why couldn't he control it?

"That's not my answer to give you. Devon should be back shortly. He has all the answers you need. I can say one thing you'll appreciate hearing."

"What's that?"

"Your body has amazing healing properties. No other person I know can do what you can."

No other hybrid, he thought. As much as he liked Annie, he still found cause to be irritated. *Hybrid. Say it, Annie. Wolf man, canine critter, utter freak.*

And likely in big trouble for whatever he did to Samey Borat.

SURPRISINGLY, DEVON arrived back at the apartment still on crutches, delivered by a hospital orderly who exited as soon as he was inside.

"Hey, kiddo," he called when he saw Garik at the table. "Life's looking up."

"Right," Garik said. "I thought the crutches were last week's news."

"The cast was step one." Devon shrugged and laid his crutches aside. He limped to the table and pulled out a chair. "Where's Annie?"

"Getting dressed. She said that since I'm awake, she wants to talk to you about her plans. I told her I didn't mind if she stayed here, and she said it's her job. She postponed her flight to help you out."

"And for that I thank you." He dropped his voice. "She cooks so well I might want her to stay forever."

"I heard that. Makes it a good time for me to make my exit." Annie appeared with her suitcase packed. "And you'll be glad to have your closet back."

"No, I won't." He winked at Garik before pulling himself to his feet to give her a kiss.

"You, sir, sit back down. They'll expect you to stay off that leg and soak it twice a day. I've been in touch with the nurses, so I know, and I'll be checking in with Garik. You're too important to me to not take care of yourself."

"She's never said that before." Devon grinned.

"Devon, Annie said you could tell me why the last day disappeared for me."

"And he wants to know about his too-small pajamas. Tell him that story, too. I'm gone. The airport calls. Bye, guys." Annie clicked out the handle on her suitcase and was gone out the door.

"So, Devo?"

"Get me some food and I'll spill it all."

IT TURNED out that Garik did fight Samey, and Samey gave Garik a good fight. His size and strength were an even match. Garik was faster. Afterward was when it got interesting. Garik leaped the ropes and went after Halo Sunchaser.

"I did that?" He was surprised not to be on Level 5 and packaged up for shipment out of the Tower.

"Rodheimer saved her by zapping you with a bolt of electricity. Even then, you didn't want to go down."

"So why am I here and not on Level 5 or locked up?"

"I don't know." Devon shrugged, pushed a biscuit in his mouth, and talked around it. "But Sunchaser seemed pleased, not angry. She was the one that stood up for you with the Director. When you wouldn't wake, Annie offered to be your nurse, and here you are."

"And the pajamas?"

"That, kiddo, you *really* don't want to know." Devon grinned and shoved another biscuit in his mouth, and he refused to give in no matter how much Garik pleaded.

$$- 5 -$$

T

his is the real reason I convinced Annie to take you in last night." Devon had a second slice of bacon in his hand, and he bit off the end.

"The real reason?" Garik looked across the table.

"Seriously?" Devon chewed and smirked at him.

"What ... oh, yes, I still repeat things." Garik stood, carried several empty dishes to the sink, and dropped them in. They clattered as they settled. He ran water over them and turned it off. He was using the time to process. Sunchaser. Rodheimer. Samey. "How bad was Samey hurt?"

"Oh, don't worry about Samey. Here, I have another plate for you." Devon slid it across the table Garik's direction.

"So, he's not hurt." He took the plate.

"Are you kidding? He was out cold, but he got in a few good punches." Devon stood, limped to the counter, held it and paused, then limped the three steps to the couch. He lifted his leg to the coffee table, worked a pillow under it, and leaned back, closing his eyes.

"Enough!" Garik's patience fractured. He slammed the plate on the counter, and it shattered in his hands. "I wake up in a place where I don't remember going to sleep, and no one spells things out. I know I'm good at figuring out most things, but sometimes I need people to tell me stuff."

Devon opened his eyes and glanced at the shattered plate. "Okay, kiddo. Is this about Samey . . . or?"

"I don't know Samey. I mean, I fought him, I guess, and I care that I didn't hurt him, so it is, but—" He felt his frustration bleed from him to be replaced by a sense of loss. Childhood, innocence, his parents in Russia, his Street Strider, Muhammad, Ibn, visiting the flower shop, the way Marisa's father used to ask him to stay in the back room when Marisa was helping a customer. "I'm sorry about the plate."

"There are more plates."

"I know. I don't have control anymore. I . . . I never did this, break plates before. Never."

"I told you once about my mother. Do you remember that?"

"She died of that baseball player's disease. ALS, I think."

"One day not long before the end, she told me something. 'Deki,' she said, 'here's what I learned from all this.'"

"Deki?" Garik smiled.

"My mom's pet name for me. Get over it, kiddo. The important thing is what she said. She said, 'Before and after are two different things. Before, I was one of the best in the world. I could have won the Olympics. Everyone said so. Now, I can't even win at staying alive. Here's the thing, Deki. I'm still the same person. The before me is completely different than the now me, but I'm still the same. Remember that. Things change. There's always a before and an after, but if you, the you at the heart of you, stays the same, then before and after don't matter. You are always still you.'"

"Am I still me?" Garik wasn't sure.

"How did you feel the first time you woke up after they did the . . . *thing* to you?"

"Not different. Nothing at all." He remembered his first look into the full-length mirror in the bathroom searching for differences. "Only my hair. They shaved it off."

"You didn't feel any different?"

"Angry."

"That's not different. I've seen you angry lots, kiddo. Tell me something I don't know."

"Yeah." Had he always been so angry before? At Arik, maybe, his aunt's boyfriend. Had he ever acted out on it? He'd wanted to sometimes. He remembered being on his Street Strider after dark on Sycamore, seeing the Tower in the distance with its façade shattering into glittering shards of silicon glitter, teasing him with its impossibility. He had wanted to be part of it so badly. Now, he was angry that he *was* part of it.

"And?"

"I had fun with my friends." At the skate park. With the three shrimpers at his apartment. With Marisa under the stars. "I lost all that."

"Like my mom said, before and after. That's life. Are you still you? What about new friends? If you had friends then . . ."

"Not the same, Devo."

"So, you don't have friends now. Poor, poor Garik, so unloved."

"You're an idiot." Garik fell into a chair across from him, lost in the before and after of his life. The change for Devon's mom had been her ALS. The change for him had been his induction into the human-hybrid program. But when had he really changed? Become so angry? Started losing part of who he was?

"And you can say that to me, and I'm not upset with you." Devon pushed the coffee table with his good leg and the corner bumped Garik's foot.

"Thank you."

"And Annie postponed her flight to help take care of you."

"Okay." Garik understood what Devon was trying to do.

"And Kofi says—"

"I get it. It's not the same."

"And it never would be, even if you weren't in here. You'd graduate, move on, leave people behind."

"But Marisa—" He stopped, his memories clogging his thoughts with what might have been.

"Change of tactics. Differences then and now. Let's make a list. Number one, uglier." Devon kept his face straight. Leaning his head back, he peered at him through half-closed eyes.

"Shut up. I feel lousy enough already."

"So, you agree, ugly is number one."

"Taller. That's number one." That was the most obvious, but Garik knew the list was a lot longer than just his height.

"Your hair's back, twice, I might add."

"I've always had that." He ran a hand over his head, remembered it long enough to tie into a knot at his neck.

"Forget that, then. Name me something else."

Running. He was fast, even without the rainbows. Endurance. Nothing much tired him. He could hear most anything, even someone's heartbeat—and he could tune it out, thank goodness. And smells, they were like flavor to him, the things he could unwrap from them.

"Eyeshine. I see pretty well in the dark."

"Number two, night vision. Is that so bad?"

"I guess not. I hear better, too."

"And how's that working?"

"I can tune it out mostly, but I hear things I'm not supposed to."

"I remember." Devon laughed. "Do you recall that first day on the climbing wall? You knew everything Vang and Dr. Jamie were saying about you, and they had no idea."

"Yeah." Garik grinned.

"That's three. Go on. Maybe those shoulders. That's different. You've become a beast—"

Garik cut a hard look to him.

"Sorry. Poor choice of words. A machine, how's that? Two other things I've noticed not on your list. The way you walk and hold your head."

"You're trying to make me feel better, right?" Garik looked at him, waiting on an explanation.

"You remember the boxer Muhammad Ali, don't you?"

"Of course. I'm not stupid."

"You said it. Not me." Devon grinned. "Float like a butterfly. He used to say that. That's you, now, the way you walk."

"My head's not a butterfly. No wings, either."

"No. But you never used to cock it to the side when you were listening. You don't even know when you're doing it."

"I can stop." Garik realized he was doing it then, and he straightened his head.

"I saw that, and no, you can't. Before and after. This is after. Figure it out. Accept what you can't change and run with it."

"What did your mom accept?"

"And there's part of the new Garik, able to turn my counseling session back on me. My mom . . . let me take a moment to sort it out." He paused for a time then continued. "She accepted that she could never ski again, that she would never see her grandchildren—"

"You'd better talk to Annie about that." Garik grinned.

"My turn to say shut up. Back to Mom, she focused on protecting me, I think. Making sure I knew she cared about me, and even though she wouldn't always be there, I would always know she loved me."

"You were her pack."

"I don't get that." Devon pulled himself erect.

"Her family, the one she wouldn't abandon ever, that she would take care of no matter what happened to her."

"Yeah, that's it." Devon smiled. "You described her exactly. That's how she was before she got sick, and her sickness didn't take that from her. She was still my mom, even when life was as bad for her as it could get."

Devon seemed caught up in his memories. After a few minutes, Garik asked, "What's the plan for today?"

"This." Devon patted the leg that was now cast-free. "I need a babysitter. Care to apply for the job?"

"AM I KICKED out of Jantzen's apartment?"

"Should you be?" Devon was on his Segway, and Garik had found his ZBoard still on its charging station in Devon's apartment.

"I thought with Rodheimer angry with me . . ." He was unforgiving when people went against his wishes. His anger at Jantzen had proven that.

"That's one of our stops today. You get to apologize." Devon slowed his Segway and turned to focus on Garik. "He has no patience for errors, but if you apologize, he wants to give second chances."

"He said that about Jantzen, only Ms. Sunchaser took away Jantzen's options."

"You and Jantzen must have hit it off. What Halo did was sketchy, but it really hit you hard. Any thoughts on that?"

"None I want to share." *He was like my father!*

"Your call, kiddo. About Annie—"

"You and Annie must have hit it off," Garik teased, to change the subject as much as anything else.

"Enough about that. With her gone, we'll be eating back in the cafeteria. We're on an assigned schedule since Brace's takeover. We'll have to plan around that. We need to get you onto the schedule with me if you stay."

"Sure. If I still have the apartment, you could come there. It has two bedrooms and two bathrooms." He liked the idea of a separate bathroom.

"Who would cook? No Annie, remember."

"Order up from the Grill." All at no charge, too.

"And miss out on cafeteria dining?" Devon chuckled.

At least, Devon pointed out, the military escorts around the research center, especially to and from meals, had been rescinded. Once Brace felt fully in control, he had let the facility return to a semblance of normality.

As if anything in the Corona Tower research facility approached anything resembling normality.

"HMM." The Director's guttural greeting vibrated, a rumbling, jarring noise, and it felt more ominous than a sharp rebuke. He addressed himself to Garik. "You are mobile today. I assumed you would recover."

Devon and Garik had waited in the main lobby. They had not, notably, been invited into Rodheimer's office, a slap of disapproval for Garik's precocious actions the previous day.

"I apologize for my lack of control, Director Rodheimer." Devon had coached Garik on exactly what to say. "I was disrespectful to Ms. Sunchaser, and I appreciate you intervening before I could injure her. Devon has been very kind to look out for me, and he assures me he can teach me coping skills so that it will never happen again."

Devon glared at Garik. The last part Garik had ad libbed.

"Understood. Halo was very forgiving, and for that, I accept your apology. Charity has your passkey to your apartment. Devon, a good deal of effort has been made to keep our young man out of mischief. Are you certain you are up to this?"

Devon, now caught in a catch-22 between Garik's lie and the Director's expectation only had one choice.

"Of course, Director. No more mischief. I promise."

"Then that's done." The Director turned and walked away.

"You promise?" Garik hissed the question.

"Teach you coping skills?" Devon returned the gibe. "Only if I can get you to listen."

"Not likely." Garik grinned and headed to retrieve his passkey.

— 6 —

D

evon's next planned stop was on Basement Level 3 where the soundproof training cells and the natatorium were located. The elevator from the main lobby in the Corona Tower stopped at Level 2 on the way down. Second Lt. Ron Wilder and Senior Airman Shan Vang joined them.

"Lieutenant. Airman." Devon recognized them and was courteous but not overly friendly.

Garik was even less so. He remembered a time

when they hadn't known he could hear them. *Mongrels, every one.* Garik didn't have a high opinion of the two men. He stood behind them, noted how much taller he was now, and framed a retort in his head if they decided to make critical remarks about him.

They remained on as Devon and Garik exited, and just before the door closed, Garik heard Wilder remark to Vang, "Who's the big guy?" Garik thought of his hair—now grown out—and the good clothes he wore. With his new height and larger frame, they hadn't known it was him.

He smiled.

"What are you happy about?"

"Those two guys in the elevator. They didn't know who I was."

"And why does that make you happy?"

"No reason. It just does."

Devon didn't spend time on it and instead headed his Segway past the Level 3 cafeteria, where several pockets of people sat together, a couple with food but most visiting, past the training cells, and to the natatorium.

"Have you met Chad?" Devon hit a switch on the wall, and the door opened electrically.

"That's new," Garik said, "and yes, if his last name is Sherwin."

Chad Sherwin had been hybridized with bat DNA, but his transformation had outpaced the Tower's parameters for a successful hybridization. He could no longer pass for human, with wing-like arms and atrophied legs. His ability to echolocate in the dark was invaluable, so he had received functional prosthetic arms and new grafted-on legs.

Twenty surgeries later, he was still restricted to his electric wheelchair.

Chad's most unusual feature was his speech. He could communicate only in the high-pitched chirps and squeals of a bat. He spoke into a translation device, which always interpreted his words as polite and well-mannered, even when Chad was not.

"Chad's in the pool today. He's one of my most impressive successes. Follow me in."

The humidity in the room felt good. It softened the air, although it didn't mute the sounds. Various people touting numerous adaptations were about, many in the water, a number not. Several were being coached, by whom, Garik didn't know. The oddest person was a misshapen lump submerging and surfacing about a person's length from the edge. It surfaced, and a box on a small stool spoke.

"So, it's true. You did make a second escape . . . and found your way back again." The words from the box were perfectly enunciated and flawlessly correct, but the thing in the water was clearly laughing at Garik.

"I don't see you flying out the door." Garik jerked his chin up, a reverse nod, letting the water creature know it had his attention.

"Because they stole my wings and gave me those. Look on the chair."

Beside the stool with the box, a pair of prosthetic arms were jumbled into a pile. Off to the side, a top-of-the-line Invacare Storm Series electric chair was charging by an outlet.

"I thought you two knew one another." Devon put his hand on Garik's shoulder to steady himself and leaned down to work his pants off his feet. He had on red trunks underneath. He tossed the pants and his shirt onto Chad's mechanical arms. Devon's Nordic heritage painted both legs lily white, but the one fresh from the cast was thinner and dry. "I have to soak the leg twice a day. This is soak one. Hold on while I drop in." Devon held Garik's arm until he was solidly over the water then let go and hit the surface with a splash.

GARIK REFUSED to change and join them, despite them pressuring him to do so. Instead, he wandered to the door, looked out to the people making their way to the training cells, some people he recognized but didn't know, a few he'd met a couple times, and Stephen Klandermans. He glanced back at Devon to find him floating next to Chad, and he slipped through the door.

"Stephen," he called. "Wait up."

"Hey, Garik!" The man raised a hand and flashed a bright smile. His gray eyes—similar to Garik's, only without the gold flecks—crinkled, and he pushed aside a thick tangle of kinky blond hair in wiry dreads. His tattered clothing—by choice—covered wide shoulders, and medicinal amulets lived in his hair. He carried a crisp ice smell of arctic purity, likely from his narwhal DNA base.

"You work with Kevin, right?"

"Sure as rice on toast. And hey, I'm sorry about Jantzen. Can't believe they let that happen to him. You two were like that." He crossed two fingers and let them slip past one another. "The man didn't deserve his end, even if he was a little off sometimes."

"I appreciate that, Stephen." The condolence tripped up Garik for a second. *A little off*, whatever that meant, but he had another question to ask. "Have you seen him today?"

"Now, like in about ten minutes. Jujitsu-nastics. My creation. Kevin teaches me jujitsu, and I add in gymnastics moves. You want to come watch?"

"I can't. I'm with Devon—"

"How's the man doing?" His expression shifted. "Hey, Dev won't mind. Come on—"

"Really, I can't. He's with Chad right now—"

"I'm there. Little Chad, that's a sad story. What can I help you with about Kevin?"

"I just—" and he didn't know what to say. Hello? I miss you? You knew Marisa and no one else did? "Just tell him I'm looking forward to our next session."

"Okay. I'll tell him just that." Stephen frowned like it didn't make any sense. He threw an arm over Garik's shoulder and pulled him in, looked side to side, then spoke low. "That sword thing? You know that was only the second time the woman has used it in public. And none of us got to see the first time. We don't mean to disrespect Jantzen, but seeing it was top of the radar. So, if we go *cool*, we're not saying cool to what happened to your man, just cool seeing the sword in action. You good with that?" He patted Garik on the chest with the flat of his palm.

"I'm good, Stephen."

"Then I got to go. I'll say your words to Kevin. You're a good man, Garik. Peace out to you." He hit him on the chest with his hand balled into a fist this time and took off.

Garik watched him go, got brushed by several people moving through the corridor, and headed back to the pool. Through the doors, the repeated sound of swimmers stroking the water and the occasional splash reverberating from the ceiling gave the place a melancholy feel.

Devon called, "Get in, kiddo. Extra suits are in the locker room."

Garik sighed, thought of Kevin and Stephen and jujitsu-nastics and Jantzen and Marisa and respect and disrespect and *even if he was a little off sometimes.* What had Stephen meant? And how was Jantzen *his man*? He looked down, crossed his fingers, and shook his head. He wasn't even sure what that meant.

He looked out across the pool. It was big, and whole lanes were unused. At the bottom, no one could hear him think, and he didn't have to listen to what anyone else thought.

"Thanks, Devo. I will."

"Right-o, kiddo!" Devon shot him a thumbs up and splashed water his direction.

"About time, loser," the tin box teased in its polite, well-mannered voice.

UNDERWATER.

Warmth. Quiet. The overhead lights creating ripples of alternating shadow and brightness across the pool floor. The occasional muffled splash of someone breaking the surface. The distant fountain of bubbles dragged along behind the person as they paddled their hands, flippers, or fins to glide through the water to the side.

And none of us got to see the first time.

Everyone saw the sword in use the first time Garik returned to the Tower. Very publicly as a hybrid was punished by being eaten alive by the white-hot surge of the electrified blade. What had they not seen? When had Sunchaser used the sword that no one had been around to view it?

Even Rodheimer had validated Stephen's remarks. Before Sunchaser brought Garik's world crashing down, when Jantzen was still alive, with Justin Kurtew and Alyna Lindberg attempting to rescue him, Rodheimer had insisted, *"Halo, you cannot continue to use the sword this way."*

Cannot continue . . . *what else had she done with it?* What other terrible thing had she done that was so distasteful that even the Director would try to steer her away from it?

Someone appeared in front of him. Devon, blond hair, the quirky cowlick at his left temple frozen even as his hair swirled in the water. Red shorts at his waist sliding against his skin, shifting position, brushing his legs in a different place. A hand, thumb up, jerking. Then Devon shooting upward, hands paddling, one leg kicking, the other hanging.

What had he wanted? Devon . . . Devo . . . his friend, his roomie, the man who listened to him, didn't judge him, yet was no longer like him. Devon was . . . Devon, still ordinary, still human, still . . . Devon.

And Garik, what was he? Human? Hardly. Two legs, yes, and two arms, and a head with a nose, ears, eyes, and a mouth. But then . . . an oversized heart, lungs he could fill with an hour's worth of air, muscles that could run without stopping. And the rainbows changing the world, lifting him out of time, moving faster than the events around him, becoming a shadow in the real world, a mere thought, before releasing the rainbows into the void and becoming Garik once more.

And where was the void that swallowed him when the rainbows took control? It was out there, a black hole of time and experience that was lived by the other Garik, the one he could never know, never contact, never *feel*.

A hand, Garik's view blurred by despair, a blond head of hair swirling in the water in front of him, fingers gripping his arm, tugging, pulling him upward, Garik struggling, not wanting to give up the peacefulness of the water. Desperate not to lose the serenity of the underwater world where he was himself and no one else, and he could be who he was meant to be.

Garik and only Garik.

Not a hybrid mutant thing with incisors and claws and a howl that would chase the full moon month after month.

His face broke the surface of the water, the warmth of the pool streamed from his skin, air scraped down his cheeks, and arms pulled him from the water.

"Garik, breathe, man!"

"Turn him over. What were you thinking, kiddo?"

Garik's chest convulsed, and he felt the water pour from his mouth. He turned on his side, coughed, realized the water had replaced the air in his lungs. He hadn't needed to return to the surface. His lungs had adapted to his environment, exactly what his abductors had bred them to do. It was refilling them with air that hurt each time he coughed.

He rolled to his back, looked around, and found the crumpled man named Chad. Then Devon, his face reflecting his panic. And Stephen.

"Stephen," he called, his voice still harsh from the coughing. When he knelt, Garik grabbed his shirt and pulled him down. "The first time. When was the first time?"

"I don't understand." Stephen frowned, and Garik yanked hard on his shirt.

"The sword. When did she use it the first time?"

"On some shop, a place on Sycamore, I think. The whole place went up in flames."

Garik let go and closed his eyes. To draw him in. That's why Sunchaser had done it. She had used the sword on The Flower Shop knowing Marisa couldn't stay away, and he would be wherever Marisa was found.

Tears or pool water, it didn't matter. Who could tell? They were for Marisa, and he let them flow.

D

evon's apartment was dark, but determination heightened the eyeshine in Garik's eyes. He lifted the passkey from Devon's bedside table, accepting the offering as the gift it was.

No regrets. Never any regrets, not where Halo Sunchaser, Marisa Bruni, and the devastation that had become Garik's life were concerned.

Now, he intended to break out of the electronic cage the Director had built around him, even if temporarily, and find out what he wasn't being told. John Carter and Paul Gberie, last seen crumpled on the parking garage floor, taken out by Luis Rodrigo's weapon. Jantzen eaten by Sunchaser's electrified sword. Giselle Harmon, Julia Cantos, Paolo Leveen, pulled from Jantzen's wrecked SUV after Sunchaser bombarded it with a sonic blast to prevent Jantzen from sublimating from solid to gas, the only way to capture a man who could escape from anything less than a hermetically sealed room.

The sound wave—a true sonic boom created by artificially induced lightning—had broken windows and peeled away the top layer of nearby sidewalks and done who knew how much damage to the three friends Garik hoped still survived in the research center hospital on Basement Level 4. He intended to find answers to the questions no one would even allow him to ask.

He inserted Devon's passkey into his computer, gifting him wider access to the research center's database than his own limited one would provide, though not much wider. That required Devon's thumbprint on the passkey, and while Garik's eyeshine might allow him to rifle through Devon's bedroom for his passkey while the activities director slept, he couldn't very well bring the man's thumb with him to fully log into the computer.

Now, he scrolled down a list of available computer workstations, part of a closed communication system within the research center's thick, underground walls. He hadn't realized there were so many people, or at least computers. He only needed one. A smaller window popped up, offering him help. He read, *Would you like me to search the database for your contact? Upload the information you have.* A box inside the window appeared with a blinking cursor.

Klandermans, he typed. *Stephen.* Before he pressed enter, he added, *Hybrid*, and *Narwhal*. That was all he knew for sure. He held his finger over the key, cringed at the thought that alarms might ring or security might show up at the door. He was risking Devon's safety, job, and reputation doing this, but it had to be done.

He clicked and nothing happened for a moment. Then, the screen said, *Accessing Stephen Klandermans. Stephen is online and accepting messages. Continue?* Yes and No appeared on the screen, and he clicked on Yes.

Words scrolled across the screen. *Hey, Dev. Late but guess you knew I'd be up. How's the new kid? Talked to him today, but you know that. Did he survive his baptism in the pool? Ha, ha. What can I do for you, man?*

Garik glanced at the passkey—Devon's—and understood why no alarms had gone off. He typed, *New kid here. Want to have an adventure?*

"SO, YOU'VE got a *tracking device* inserted in you?"

Stephen grinned. "Inserted, like, *where?*"

"Not anywhere I can easily remove it. The Director made that clear. That's why I have to have Devon's passkey, and that's why we have to be back before he wakes up. I need you because his passkey won't get me anywhere without a way to bypass the palm scanners."

"And I'm your palm scanner friend." Stephen smiled broadly. "Can't waste time, then. You are a sneaky one. I like that."

Stephen was pretty sneaky himself. The research campus ran on an aboveground schedule, with a full night for most people. Cleaning crews and night owls roamed the dimmed corridors but bumping into someone who knew them was unlikely. Still, Stephen had his dreadlocks bundled into a knit cap and wore a gray tracksuit rather than his usual tattered threads. No simple glance would connect the ordinary man walking past with the outrageous Stephen Klandermans.

Garik was dressed in a nod to Jantzen in a black hooded shirt pulled around his face with his hands covered by black gloves. It was the Jantzen from the food court screens from before he had gotten to know him. It was a stretch that they were anything alike, what with Jantzen's beard and Garik's height, but with his dark brown hair a black shadow under the hood, it gave Garik a sense of purpose that they might.

Garik's first goal was to infiltrate the hospital. Find out about Giselle, Julia, and Paolo. They had escaped with Garik the first time he'd managed to get away, certain they were being phased out of the program. That meant Level 5, possibly in cages to allow DNA or body parts to be harvested before being shunted to whatever final destination was planned for those no longer viable for use.

If they were considered beyond use then, why nurse them back to health now? Garik's only conclusion was that the researchers wanted to monitor the recovery rate of a hybridized body when subjected to excess shock waves. Liver pulverized . . . how long until a new one grows? Blood vessels ruptured . . . could the body reroute the blood flow quickly enough? Soft membranes, heart structure, even the eyes? What parts of the damaged body would recover . . . and would they be better or worse afterward? Perhaps sonic shock waves were a new way forward, the trigger to initiate the change from one level of development to the next in a newly hybridized body.

Jantzen had said the Director took six months to achieve his final form. Garik considered himself: no changes at first, then wham! and look at him now. Kevin had called him a beast, then changed it to a machine. Then and now. Before and after. Sonic boom, the shockwave that triggers the new and different hybrid to erupt from the human it had been.

What was his sonic boom? What vital thing had happened to him that vaulted him from a boy to a beast? From ordinary to something more?

Something had triggered him to suddenly accelerate his changes from human to hybrid. He needed to work out what. Information, evaluation, extrapolation. Not precognition or prescience. Rather, he would gather information efficiently, match it all together like a puzzle, and see the possible outcomes like a tree laid out before him. The main trunk revealed what was about to happen, then primary branches, each with equal possibilities, and then smaller branches diverging off those, each possible, but each less probable the further he looked along the tree.

Now, Garik gathered. Stephen was with him because Garik had seen down the path without him, and his search had collapsed into disaster every time.

"Listen." Garik touched Stephen's arm. "Now, into here." A short corridor gave access to three doors, none of which were open, but the recess got them out of the sight path along the main corridor.

"I don't hear—"

"Shh!" Garik placed a hand just in front of Stephen's mouth. *Not a sound*, he mouthed.

"Down this way." A familiar voice, Airman Shan Vang, a man who had little patience with Garik and had at one time suggested he was a failed hybrid and should be disposed of.

Airman Vang, Garik mouthed to Stephen. Stephen frowned doubtfully, then the diminutive Vang stepped briskly down the corridor followed by two of Colonel Brace's hybridized paramilitary goons in full blacked-out gear, including helmets with oxygen concentrators on the faceplates, their one flaw, and what the Tower was trying to overcome to create a more perfect super soldier with no flaws at all.

"They're gone," Garik said softly. "Vang hates me. He'd know something was up for sure."

"And you heard him. Wolf, I know, but you hear that well?"

"And smell even better. I can smell the last thing you ate on your fingers."

"What I ate?" He sniffed his fingers.

"Yeah. Squid, and you like them raw."

"And the rest of me?" Stephen chuckled. "Better or worse?"

"Better. Arctic ice. I like the way you smell." Garik stepped to check the corridor and finding it clear, motioned Stephen forward.

"What's so great about arctic ice?"

"No smell at all, just cold and brisk. Pure. I don't have to think when I smell you, well, except for your fingers." Garik grinned.

"Idiot." Stephen didn't seem particularly irritated. He pulled out his passkey. "Elevator. Hospital, here we come."

He inserted it, palmed the door, and they stepped inside. He reinserted it into the inside panel, pushed the icon for Level 4, and the car began to move.

GARIK WAS surprised to find Level 4 fully lighted and filled with activity.

"I thought the hospital would be shut down at night. Well, the lights turned down, anyway."

"Nah, man. This is their busiest time. All the crazy stuff. The rest of us are in bed, and they don't have to hide anything they do."

"You couldn't tell me?" His three friends. He was this close.

"See, I knew it might take the edge off, and I didn't want to dampen your excitement. I also know that where there's a will, there's a way. I work down here some, and my passkey is cleared. I have a back door in." Stephen took Garik's arm and pulled him along a secondary corridor with minimal activity. Once, they passed an orderly who nodded at them, asked if she could help, and when Stephen shook his head, went about her business with no suggestion they shouldn't be there.

Stephen's back door took them to a storage area. For reference, he explained that it was underneath the research labs two floors above, and that was just under the research center's main lobby where the hybrid family had gathered the time Sunchaser had "demonstrated" her electrified sword.

Garik remembered. He had watched a woman be

dismembered by the sword's beam of pure lightning . . . molecule by molecule . . . atom by atom. He shivered at the power it contained to be able to do something so awful. He glanced at the ceiling. "So, the sword is stored in the research labs."

"Why would you think that?" Stephen was navigating racks, bins, and long corridors, many with indecipherable equipment, but also with paper goods and cleaning supplies.

"It dropped into the floor. It makes sense—"

"Nothing around here makes sense, man. It drops all the way down, comes *here*, to *storage*. Deep storage is safe storage. Wanna see the room?"

"Yes." He didn't have to even think about it. The sword. Marisa's sword, the one she had drawn on her MicroArt tablet. It wasn't hers, of course, but it had fascinated her, and she had scoured the Internet to learn everything about it. She had always felt there was something in the schematics the Tower had never released—a missing layer—and if it could be found . . .

Stephen opened a door with his passkey, unmarked except for B4-ES. A light clicked on as they entered. Inside was a small room with shelves along the sides. A heavy-duty door faced them with a wire-infused glass window.

"There," Stephen pointed.

"We can get to it?" Garik looked through the glass, rested his hand on the handle, and gave it a try. It didn't budge. On the other side, in the darkness, the glass case he had seen once before with the sword resting inside, glinting with the light leaking in from the small window. "I don't see the steel vault."

"No one gets in there without the big brass in attendance. The vault stays on Level 2. I'd turn the lights on and let you have a better look, but there's no switch out here."

"That's okay." The shadowed ceiling with a seam down the middle. Scissor arms to open it. The lighting, now dark, recessed into the walls. He didn't tell him he could see inside just fine.

"Come. Let's check in on your three friends. Make sure they are in one piece. Has anyone ever told you we're pretty hard to kill? If they brought them down still alive, they'll likely pull through."

Unless they are blown apart by a bullet or disintegrated by a bolt of lightning spewed out by an electrified sword. Other than that, sure, Stephen. We're pretty hard to kill.

He hoped the man was right. For his friends' sakes. Death was too permanent, and he was tired of it happening to people he knew.

He almost said loved, but Jantzen hadn't hung around long enough for that. And nothing had filled the hollow he'd left behind. He expected nothing could, except perhaps a good dose of revenge.

— 8 —

think that's Julia," Garik whispered, motioning to a bed with a tall form, although the monitoring equipment and the low lights might make it difficult for anyone else to make out her identity.

"In one piece, it seems," Stephen agreed.

Garik had tagged behind through the unfamiliar corridors once they reemerged in the underbelly of the hospital. It was the middle of the night, and the ward they entered consisted of glass-fronted rooms arranged around a central nurse's station, typical of many ICUs. The lights were down except just at the station.

"Can I help you?" The nurse had been reading a paper book, and he turned it upside down to mark his place and stood. The ward was silent, with blinking lights revealing life-monitoring machines in most of the glass-fronted rooms. Two were completely dark, suggesting they were empty.

"We're checking up on some old friends."

"This late?" The nurse wasn't unfriendly, just questioning.

"I can't get out easily during the day. My eyes, understand." Stephen had pulled out a pair of tinted goggles and slipped them over his face despite the dim lights. "I brought my friend to help me navigate the brighter areas. If you think it's best that we come back . . ." He let his enquiry trail away as if the nurse was right to turn him away, but it would be devastating if he did.

"Of course. I should have noted that. And you are?"

"Stephen, and my friend is Kiddo." Stephen glanced at Garik and gave him a wink. "We can offer our passkeys as verification." He held out his and motioned to Garik to do the same.

"Sure. Here." Garik held up one, unsure if it was his or Devon's.

"Let me see—" He reached for Stephen's passkey, paused, looked at his desk, and said, "No, that's okay.

You won't be able to visit, anyway. As you can see, everyone's resting. I can give you a verbal review on them. Who are you interested in?"

"Julia, for sure," Stephen said. He pointed to the bed Garik had indicated. "That's her, there."

"You can see that?" The nurse paused, then he smiled. "Right, your eyes. You said friends. Who else?"

Garik leaned in and whispered, "Giselle Harmon and Paulo Leveen. Julia's last name is Cantos."

"Giselle Harmon, Paulo Leveen, and Julia's last name is Cantos."

The nurse frowned at the recited list of names before looking at his screen. "Okay, all here. Let me look at their progress . . . not surgery . . . ah, internal injuries, monitoring only. Hmm, this says . . ." He looked up, impressed. "Readings are off the charts. It seems your friends are making good progress. At this rate, I don't see any apparent cause for concern. Quite the opposite."

"They're okay, then." Garik still held the passkey, by now gripped tightly in one hand.

"I'm just the night nurse, so I haven't personally attended them, but the reports say so." He picked up his book to indicate an end to their visit. "Then, that's hybrids for you. You'll need to know they are in induced comas, so even if you return tomorrow, they won't know you. Call in next time, and that will save you a visit. Have a good night."

"I NEED access to the mainframe."

"You need . . . what?" They were back in the elevator, and Stephen, even with his penchant for boldness, gave Garik a look of amazement.

"Yes." They had passed by door B4-ES on the way out, and while they hadn't stopped, Garik hadn't been able to get the sword and the impact it had made on his and Marisa's lives out of his head. If he could learn more about it, maybe discover the hidden schematics Marisa said were missing, it would be like giving her something back, finishing a dream that had been stolen from her.

"I don't have access to the mainframe, man. How are you planning to do that?"

"I'm working on it." Which meant he didn't have a plan, only hoped to think of one. He pictured the ICU and thought of the nurse's words. The sonic boom, had it been instrumental in *improving* Giselle, Paulo, and Julia? If so, what would Jantzen have vaulted into? If he hadn't been dismembered by Sunchaser's sword, would he have become a super-hybrid, able to morph into anything he wanted, perhaps even with god-like attributes? Maybe walk through walls, X-ray vision, or live on an airless moon? Could the sword be something different, even more than they were led to believe? He asked, "What was your sonic boom?"

Stephen laughed as the elevator door opened. "I

have no idea what you mean, but I can come up with some interesting answers."

"I'm sorry." Garik had so much in his head, and he forgot others couldn't follow everything he was thinking. "The thing that caused you to be like you are."

"My mother and my father got married . . ."

"C'mon." Garik smiled. They were in the corridor, and they were forced to keep their voices down. The night was coming to a close, and more people were moving about, some dressed for early training, others using the corridors as a convenient jogging track. The breakfast crowd would emerge in waves in another hour. "Here, when you had the procedure done. You didn't change immediately. No one does. Something must have caused you to change from who you were to who you are now."

"My magic powers, you mean."

"Yes."

"Sorry, I didn't get any. My special power is all about bone density. Space travel, all that. I can't see it or feel it, but the doctors seem to think it's important. The rest of me is how I've been all my life."

"Oh, sorry."

"I'm not sorry. I like me."

"I didn't mean it that way. I, well, I wasn't any different for a long time, then everything became different. My before and my after. I need to find what came in the middle."

"Your catalyst. That's what you're looking for. Man, I know how you feel. Like when I wanted to do gymnastics. Everybody laughed, but I'd seen the Olympics on television, and I knew I could compete and take gold. I was inspired."

"I didn't know you competed." Garik thought of Devon's mom who'd never had the chance for gold.

"Nah, but I could. Well, not now, but I could."

"So, you'll help me?" Garik felt the pressure of needing to get Devon's passkey back, but this was as important. He was risking their friendship, but to not take the risk meant leaving a personal hole in who he was, and that was worse.

Protecting himself. Protecting the pack. Which would win in the end?

"RISKY BUSINESS," Stephen said when he and Garik passed each other in the corridor later that morning. He slipped a folded piece of paper into Garik's hand and leaned in, lips to ear, to say, "Eat it when you're done, sooner than later."

Garik did, memorizing the filched passcode, and now he sat immersed in exploring the Tower's mainframe, searching, searching. Risky business indeed, as he was in Devon's apartment. He was certain his searches could be traced back to here if someone looked. He hoped no one did.

He didn't have access to *everything*, but then he

hadn't wanted or needed that. He hoped to find out about the electrified sword, check out the research lab records on hybrid transformation rates, and if possible see what they had on him. What had they recorded that they hadn't shared, the thing that made the Director so willing to give him second chances and for Sunchaser to be pleased that he had leaped from the boxing ring to attack her?

He had pleaded tiredness after lunch—true after his all-nighter—and asked to be left in the apartment. Devon offered to bring something from the emergency clinic, but no, Garik had assured him rest was all he needed. By the time Devon left, he was in his pajamas.

He had, however, no intention of sleeping.

PROPOSALS. Committee meeting reports. Financial documentation. Job openings. Military assignments. The categories of information seemed endless.

Then, case studies, and Garik knew he was moving in the right direction. He clicked to open, and names flooded down the screen. He looked for ones that were familiar, Paolo, Giselle, Julia, and there they were. John Carter—

Garik's emotions hiccupped. John, left face down on the parking garage floor. Pointless.

He scrolled by Stephen Klandermans' file, refusing to open it. Stephen had passed him the code to access this information. Snooping wasn't why he was here, at least not snooping into Stephen's files.

Marina, Marisa's sister. A red X. He opened it. She had been transferred out of the complex, sent away to some distant location. He searched for where, only to see a series of letters and numbers that meant nothing to him.

Then Jantzen Hefferly. The file, still open, unlike Marina's. He clicked it, and Jantzen's life spilled onto the screen. His birthdate, hometown, pictures of him before and after his involvement in the human-hybrid project. Garik found professional credentials telling that the man was not only a participant, but a medical doctor and a celebrated researcher, with mentions in too many prominent research publications to scan in the time Garik had.

One of the pictures was the photo of Jantzen attempting to pull Rodheimer off the log. Garik zoomed the image to fill the screen with the youthful face, like yet very unlike the man who had befriended him. He closed the picture. That wasn't the Jantzen he knew, only an earlier version of him. No purple eyes, no beard, none of the character that had made up Jantzen.

He caught a boldface subheading, Catalyst, the word Stephen had used. He read: *Jantzen Hefferly's hybrid transformation occurred over two stages, the second of which seems to have been precipitated by a "trigger" event. 1. His initial transformation spanned four months and was thought to be a failure. During this time, he continued his work in the research labs, although he reported increasing headaches. Multiple MRI scans found no evidence of abnormalities. 2. Jacques Ricciardo, hybrid, was reclassified as a failure and excluded from the program, creating the trigger event that enhanced Hefferly's transformation exponentially. Note: the reason for Hefferly's intense reaction to Ricciardo's reclassification is unclear, but the inescapable conclusion is that severe emotional stress can accelerate the change into full hybrid state.*

Garik forced himself to consider, could his own emotional trauma have forced him to change? He swelled with missing Marisa, certain the two must be connected. He closed Jantzen's file and reopened Marina's. He scanned for Catalyst and found it. Underneath, it said, None. He looked for Benjamin Fuest, a man who seemed to have no hybrid characteristics. Catalyst: None. Then he went to Justin Kurtew, a man who had made the most extreme change he could imagine, from a person to a creature that was more mantis than man. Under Catalyst, he found something unexpected. *Jantzen Hefferly/severed relationship.*

Severed relationship. Garik had known there was something there, a sore spot, a grudge Justin held against Jantzen, almost envy for Garik's new place in Jantzen's life. What relationship fracture could have been so serious that it would trigger Justin to become what he was now?

And Dr. Jimenez's comment on the mall when he'd seen Garik with Jantzen. Garik had surprised him, but when Jantzen said they were together, the doctor had said, "Then I'm not surprised."

He also thought of Stephen, the crossed fingers, his reference to Jantzen as "his man." And when Justin was molting, Jantzen had been there to help him, caring friends. None of it made any sense.

Then something he was reading clicked. At the bottom of Marina's file had been a code telling where she was transferred. He reopened Jantzen's file, and in parenthesis, as if not official, was the same code. What did that mean?

He thought of the sword, what had happened to Jantzen, other people Sunchaser had hit with the electrified weapon. He searched for his own file, and he scanned it for the dreaded subheading.

Catalyst: Subject's progress has stalled. A trigger event is suggested. Strongest probable emotional connection: Marisa Bruni. Suggest severing the connection. See Jantzen Hefferly's file for a successful example.

When poisoning her against him hadn't worked, Sunchaser had upped the ante. She had killed Marisa to bring about his full hybrid transformation.

Garik knew one thing. Somehow, she would pay.

— 9 —

G

arik searched for one more thing in his file. The odd code. The rest was in there, summarized, of course, but very much reflecting his life since entering the center, even his assignment to Jantzen's apartment in the Tower and the statistics from all his training sessions.

His file had no code, the only thing that seemed to connect Marina and Jantzen. They were both no longer in the Tower. He closed the folder and went to Christian Maguire, a hybrid reject he and Jantzen had tried to save but who was ejected from the program and the Tower before their plan was complete. The blowup between Jantzen and Sunchaser over Christian had created a rift between them, with the result being Jantzen's destruction by the sword.

Christian. Red X. Inside, the mysterious code. Garik looked to his Catalyst, where it said: *No successful triggers found. Subject continues to develop at a progressive and steady rate.*

Down the list, he caught other names: Veronika Abbink; Anatoli and Andrey Burgorski. He opened that one, caught a description that said each had half a butterfly birthmark. He grinned and moved on. Fabiola Bello; Bert Ellis; Amy Howe; Leigh Jose; Laura Lassere; Marco Lopez; Hector Mascari; Jacquelien Van Kessel; and there were others. He opened Jacquelien's file, was surprised to learn that the blonde woman had African ancestry in her blood. He wanted to read more, but Devon might return at any time. Faithful, dependable Devon, out to watch over him, and good-hearted, too. Garik appreciated each of Devon's qualities, and he had come to trust him as a friend; but he needed time in the mainframe, and Devon wouldn't mesh well with that.

He scrolled, clicked when something looked promising, and entered a folder labeled Research Center Electrical Plans. All five basement floors were inside the folder with detailed drawings identifying each room. Several voids were marked Utility Access. After studying them, he closed the folder and thought for a minute. The sword. He tried to think how Marisa had accessed the information all those months ago, back when it was summer, and he was still a high school boy who had liked a high school girl, and he hadn't known the research center in the Tower's basement existed. At the top of the screen, he selected New Window, and in the search bar, he typed Corona Tower, added a slash, put in Halo Sunchaser, another slash, then added ESS. Tapping Enter brought up a list of pages, all of which told something about the electrified sword, from images to plastic toy versions for sale.

One option was labeled Corona Tower Home, and he clicked it. A picture of the sword appeared, and at the top, a series of drop-down menus. One said Schematics, and Garik clicked it. A labeled diagram of the sword appeared, and at the bottom, a tag said 1 of 59.

One of fifty-nine. Not one of sixty—an even number, which would make more sense. He flipped through the pages. Add a cover sheet, maybe a page with credits at the back. Even was complete, and the Tower never did anything in halves. He understood Marisa's declaration that the Tower must have published the schematics—required by law—but left off a page. It was too complicated to easily know if you had all of it, and just one part missing would be enough that anyone trying to build it from this would fail and likely not understand why.

Interestingly, the longer he studied the pages, the more sense it made to him. He had always been able to look at items, especially mechanical or electronic ones, and have a feel for how they worked and how to repair them. And now, hybridized, his memory was nearly photographic. In his head, he began to overlay the pages on the screen one on another, building up the finished sword in his head as he surveyed the images. By the time he was finished, he had a good grasp on what each part of the machine—and it was that, simply a machine with energy reservoirs, controls, and feedback sensors—did to make it operate.

One thing puzzled him. The sword didn't feel destructive. It felt passive, a conduit, not a rail gun for electricity. The design wanted to *channel* something.

He needed page sixty. The design wasn't finished. Thank you, Marisa, he thought, sending his appreciation to wherever she might be. I wouldn't know to keep looking, but thanks to you, now I do.

The front door to the apartment unlocked, thunk, thunk, and Devon called, "Hey, kiddo! How's your afternoon been?"

"Fine, Devo," he called back, as he logged out of his mainframe search. He didn't know if he would be able to get back in, but what he had found so far was invaluable.

"Studying?" Devon was at the door on his crutches.

His leg was mostly better, but it would be months before he would walk and run like his old self.

"Yeah. Lots of information out there."

"Don't let it suck you in. Do you feel like a trip to the cafeteria, or should we plan to eat in?"

"Out." Garik pushed away from the computer. He suddenly wanted to be away from it, out of the room, gone from the apartment. He needed to see some faces besides his own.

"I'm on the Segway. I just need a fresh shirt. Are you taking your board?"

"Of course." Garik looked beside the computer to the passkey to Jantzen's apartment that he had yet to use since the incident with Sunchaser. Two bathrooms didn't seem so important anymore. The place was large, with great views, but it didn't have the one thing this place had: Devon. Someone who would walk in the door, ask him if he wanted to go out, and be satisfied no matter how he answered.

In other words, a friend.

He followed Devon into his bedroom, and he found him in the closet, his torso bare, flipping through an assortment of hanging shirts. His old shirt was on the floor and his crutches leaned against the bed. Garik dropped into his boxing stance and threw a couple mock jabs with his fists.

"Ho, ho, watch out, Devo," he said.

"What's that for?"

"Gotta fight'cha while youse is still all cripple up. Utterwise, ain't no contest. I be losin'."

"Gotta get your head screwed on straight before I let you back into civilization. Are you wearing that to eat?" Devon pulled a shirt down, slipped it over his head, and buttoned it at the collar.

"Comfy." Garik grinned.

"Not with me, you're not. Put on some real clothes." He reached for his dirty shirt, and he popped Garik with it. As Garik ducked and ran, Devon chased after him, one footed, popping as he went, finally calling, "Ow, ow! You win."

"Always, Devo." Garik snatched the shirt from him and popped him back, before throwing the shirt at him and heading to his room for real clothes.

IN THE cafeteria, mealtimes were still assigned, so they had a good idea who they might see. Melanie Hatherill and the Burgorski twins, plus Lansana Opuku-Mensah and Jacquelien Van Kessel. Schedules could be rotated, but it took prior approval from Colonel Brace's team, and for most people, it was too much trouble.

There was no restriction about where they sat, even with Brace's men at the door checking off each person who walked in, so they tended to pull together tables for a good time. Anatoli and Andrey had already pulled two tables together, and when Garik and Devon walked in, they waved.

"Spots saved. Join in," Andrey called.

"Got a joke for you," Anatoli shouted, standing to be sure everyone heard. "A cripple and a wolf walked into a diner—"

He was booed into silence by the other attendees, and he sat with a grin on his face.

"Happy, Anatoli?" Devon had his Segway at the table, and he stepped off. He used the edge of the table for support and dropped into his seat.

"Got everyone's attention, right? Of course, I'm happy." He looked to Garik. "Three more chairs, slave. Right over there where we got the tables."

"Massa." Garik left his board with the Segway and headed across the room. From behind him, he heard Anatoli whispering, *"I heard he's wearing a tracking device."* Garik turned, and Anatoli waved, as if he hadn't said anything. He worked his arms under three chairs at once, growling to himself, *Stephen!* He couldn't believe the man would reveal something Garik had told him in what he thought was confidence.

Back at the table, Garik seated himself, and when the three women arrived, he stood beside his chair until they were seated.

"A gentleman," Jacquelien purred. She was blonde, which forced the red tattooed line running from her widow's peak down her face before disappearing into her shirt to stand out. The only thing more distinctive was her blue lips. She was willing to take a risk, and

Garik liked her for that.

Lansana, with scarification about her eyes, watched Jacquelien sit before pulling out her own chair.

Melanie had her chair out and was seated before either of the other two.

"Jacquelien," Garik said as an opener, "do you like challenges?"

"Already smells good." She rubbed her hands together. "What it is, and what do I get if I'm successful?"

"What you get is respect." Garik drummed four fingers on the table once for drama.

"Hmm," she said, looking at the other people around the table. "Whose?"

"Someone who knows something only two other people at this table know. Someone who can smash in the face of a paramilitary goon and walk away. Someone who can hear whispers from across the room." Anatoli looked at Garik sharply, and Garik thought, *Process that.* He said, "Mine."

"Ooh, so sweet a reward. I'm in. What's the challenge, and what do I lose if I can't meet it?"

"You help me find—" It came to Garik like inspiration. "—the missing schematics page for the sword."

"Shut up. It's not possible," Anatoli said.

"What schematics?" Devon looked doubtful.

"How did you—" Lansana, her eyes narrowed.

Melanie didn't say anything, but Anatoli elbowed

Andrey, and Garik found he had their full attention.

"Deal," Jacquelien said. "The challenge?"

"A butterfly landed, half on one, half on the other. Tell me where it is, the first half and the other, before we finish eating."

"Ooh, a good one." She smiled and rubbed her hands together.

Anatoli and Andrey looked intrigued until they figured out it was them, and the butterflies weren't in a location suitable for public viewing.

"Who wants pizza?" Garik stood. It was the only thing on the menu tonight. Brace hadn't relaxed *that* rule. What one person ate, everyone in the room shared.

As he walked across the room, he thought, *Let them sweat that.*

BY THE end of the meal, the twins were squirming and asking to be dismissed. The women assured them it wasn't happening. Besides, there was a guard on duty that said they were to remain in the cafeteria until their slot for dinner was up. As the brothers grew redder, Jacquelien focused on them. Matching men, half and the other, and she called them on it. When they denied it, her only solution was to ask for proof, which they declined to give.

"I suppose we must help you look for your treasure, since we've hit an impasse on your riddle." She placed her hand on Garik's and released it equally quickly.

"Anatoli and Andrey will be glad to join us."

"I can give you a hint, if that's all you want." Andrey. "It won't do you much good."

"I'm good at putting things together. Try me." Garik.

They all knew about the missing schematic. Andrey had seen the room where the only copy was kept locked away. He described the location, telling them it was behind an unmarked door, impossible to access.

Garik listened, placed the room on the electrical plans in his head, and he said, "What if it is possible?"

They rounded up a pen and opened several napkins, and Garik began to draw from his memory. Each floor, crisp and clear, and right behind the room Andrey described was a void labeled Utility Access.

"Get us in there," Garik said, "and we're in the room."

Jacquelien smiled. "I like this part even better."

Melanie joined in, "So. Do. I."

Garik smiled. The quest was on.

$-$ 10 $-$

S

eriously," Devon said, taking in the group of hybrids at the table, "you are just going to go in there, prowl around, and poke into what you shouldn't?" He shook his head. "And in the most secure facility in the country. You do know that's off limits."

"Practice." Lansana's eyes carried a look of anticipation. "Trained for this. Classes, the military instructors, all of it. What they have given us. Military-grade skills. No good if not used."

"She's got a good point." Andrey leaned back, frowning, thinking.

"I'm in, Andrey." Anatoli grinned and placed his hand on his brother's arm and removed it. Neither man seemed to notice he'd done it. "A real covert operation. Maybe even under the cover of night. Let's do this."

"Darkness. Anyway." Melanie's speech was separated into clipped sections, each seemingly independent of the other.

"Leave that to me," Garik said. He could smell the eagerness of the chase from each person at the table, all except Devon. Devon emanated hesitancy, concern for the rules of the game, worry that the current status quo, already tenuous, might topple one or all of them into a place that they wouldn't be able to rescue themselves from.

"I promised no shenanigans, kiddo. Remember?" Devon balled his hand and bumped Garik's shoulder. "Aren't you worried that this might be considered a shenanigan?"

"You're worried it might be, that's obvious," Garik said. He looked to the others at the table. "Is this a shenanigan? Devon's worried that it might be."

"I have been challenged." Jacquelien stood, sliding her chair back, and crossing her arms over her chest. "Where is my honor, my identity, if I do not meet the challenge? My grandfather was a tribal leader in my South African homeland, and I dishonor him if I do not hold to my end of any bargain I have entered into."

Lansana smiled. Melanie put her hand under her chin and studied Devon's reaction. Anatoli took one of the napkins Garik had drawn on, wadded it, and tossed it Jacquelien's direction, hitting her before it tumbled back to the table.

"Climb off your pedestal, woman. You don't have a tribal leader in your DNA. You are Dutch seahorse through and through. Look at that blonde hair."

Jacquelien glared, and Garik stepped in. "Airman Vang, anyone know him? Cambodian or Irish? Anyone? Anyone? So, leave it, Anatoli." Garik had seen the file. He knew she was telling the truth.

"Thank you." Jacquelien sat, but she glowered at Anatoli.

Devon said, "I'm not here, and I'm not hearing any of this. We had dinner, then I went to check on the emergency clinic supplies, and after that, well, I'll think of someplace that proves I wasn't with you people. Garik," he rapped the table with the knuckles of his fist, "you need a minder. How are you planning to deal with that?"

"I forgot." Garik's enthusiasm hit a wall.

Devon moved his hand, and his passkey rested on the table. "I'll be back to the apartment by nine. I'd hate to think I misplaced my passkey and couldn't get in. It might be embarrassing when security shows up, and you're nowhere around. I did promise the Director I was up to keeping you in line."

Garik covered the passkey with his hand, grinned, and said, "Lost passkey? What lost passkey?"

As Devon rose and made his way to his Segway, Garik motioned the others to pull in, and he leaned forward. He kept his voice low.

"First, we need to get to Level 4. Who wants to volunteer their passkey?"

Five hands shot into the air.

ACCESSING THE utility corridors seemed impossible at first. They tried several of the entrances Garik recalled from his view of the center's electrical plans, but none allowed them through. Their break came when Joseph Howard came down the hallway pushing a mop bucket with a wooden handle protruding from the top.

"Hey, Joseph, let me help you with that." Anatoli took off at a trot to catch the head of the center's custodial team. "You should have Tyrone doing these sweat jobs. You're his boss, you know."

"Not that Tyrone knows." Joseph Howard chuckled, and he studied Anatoli's face. "I thought that was you, Anatoli. How is that brother of yours?"

"Just down the corridor. There, see him?" He pointed.

"Sure, with the big guy. Looks familiar, that face."

"Likely. Can I hold the door for you while you roll this inside?"

"I bet you can. Let me unlock this."

With the man's passkey, the door swung wide, and Anatoli held it out of the way while the older man pushed the bucket inside.

"You need help pouring that water out?"

"I'm good with it. Thanks. I won't be needing anything else."

"I see an electrical panel behind you. It looks big enough to be a doorway."

"Yessir. Been through it a few times. A whole world behind there nobody sees but me."

"And Tyrone." Anatoli chuckled.

"When I can get him out of his lazy shoes." Joseph had the bucket empty and the mop hung to dry. "Be going now, Anatoli. You tell that brother of yours to be better than you are." He winked.

"Yessir, Joseph. I sure will."

After Joseph exited, Anatoli let the door swing to, and he pushed it firmly closed. He watched Joseph round the corner before he waved to his cohorts.

Andrey called, "C'mon, Anati, we have another location to try."

"No, *you* come on, brother. This is the way in." When they arrived, Anatoli touched the handle and the door swung open with a feather touch. Anatoli gestured to where he had slipped a magnetic plate to keep the latch from engaging. "Alarms, do I hear alarms? No? After all, what is there in a custodian's closet to steal?"

"This. Helps. How?" Melanie, her voice curt with impatience.

"I understand." Garik smiled. He had seen the electric panel, and he had already placed it on the plan in his head. It had to be a door. The path through it was as clear as if it were painted on the floor.

Actually, it was. Two lines, black and red, with voltage symbols inscribed alongside them. The lines stopped at the front of the electrical panel. Garik knew they continued on the other side.

"Jacquelien," he suggested, "check to see how to open that panel. It opens to the utility corridor."

"That's what Joseph said," Anatoli confirmed.

"A. Door." Melanie smiled.

"I told you Anati would be good for something." Andrey smirked.

"You said what?" Anatoli punched him on the shoulder. "I'm always good for something."

"If only we could figure out what it is." The electrical panel was open by then, and Andrey ducked through just before Anatoli slapped the side of his head.

THEY LEFT the electrical panel ajar, as it didn't latch from the back, and wedged the door to the corridor shut. Anyone trying it . . . but then no one would. It was locked, after all.

Garik had no trouble following the path to the room Andrey had described. The lighting was low, but the plan for the building was firmly fixed in his mind. This corridor, that one, turn there, and access that wall to gain entrance.

One thing the building's electrical plan hadn't shown was how large each electrical access was to the various rooms. The one they had entered—a full door. The one they needed to gain access to the backside of the room with the final schematic for the electrified sword? Yet another difficulty to work out in pursuit of their goal.

"This is it." Garik tapped the wall with his knuckles. A cable burrowed through concrete block and gave off a hollow thump of resonance from inside the invisible cavities.

"No. Door." Melanie, stating the obvious.

"See that." Lansana. "Need to work it out."

"Jacquelien's challenge. Let her do it." Either Anatoli or Andrey, who could tell? The corridors were darkened, or so they looked to anyone without eyeshine, and the men's faces were shadowed in the dim lights littering the edges of the floor.

"Right here?" Jacquelien drew a box shape on the wall with her hands. "We want on the other side of this spot? Are you certain?"

"Completely." Garik had walked the steps from turn to turn. He knew the distances. The picture in his head didn't lie.

"Lansana?" Jacquelien stepped back and motioned

to her.

Lansana tilted her long neck, absorbing what she must do. Then she nodded, accepting the challenge. She stepped back and slammed into the wall with her shoulder. When it didn't break, she smiled apologetically.

"Melanie," Lansana said politely. "Glancing blow. At my shoulder."

Melanie groaned then walked a hundred steps down the corridor. When she turned, Lansana crouched as if prepared to impact the wall once more. Melanie began to run, blurred, and Lansana was slammed sideways. Dust flew, and when she pulled herself erect, the concrete block bore a series of distinct cracks. Lansana with her armored pangolin skin was unharmed.

She called to Melanie, "Again."

Melanie took a deep breath, jogged to her starting position, and began to run once more.

ONCE INSIDE, the room was completely dark, with only the glow from the utility corridor to provide any light. Garik could see fine. The others needed extra illumination to keep from bumping into things.

"Okay, Andrey. You're the one that described this place. Where do we look?" If Garik were Sunchaser, and the most important document for the electrified sword's cherished schematics couldn't fall into anyone's hands, what would be the obvious place?

About the time Andrey counted drawers, Garik already knew, and they reached for it at the same time.

"Locked." Andrey groaned. "I should have known."

"Would. Be." Melanie.

"Don'tcha think?" Anatoli.

"But the challenge!" Jacquelien took Anatoli and Andrey by the ears, and she said, "This is your fault. I refuse to lose. Show the birthmarks!"

Garik laughed. "I would rather have the schematic. I've got this." He grasped the drawer pull, twisted until the front of the drawer began to buckle, then with a yank, ripped it free. A leather folder rested inside. His heart raced, and he thought, *For you, Marisa,* and he lifted it out.

Inside, the printed design that revealed the true purpose of the sword leaped out at him. It clicked into place, lining up with the other fifty-nine pages. It was obvious, so simple. The sword was never designed to kill. He was right. It was a channel, a conduit. For what he wasn't sure but leaving this part of the design incomplete caused the sword's power to short from the blade, wreaking havoc on whatever it touched.

It was obvious, and it could never be allowed to happen again. There was only one thing to do.

"I need access to the sword." Garik looked up from the schematic, and he studied each person in the room, gauging their reactions.

"Always love a good joke." Anatoli chuckled.

"The. Paper. Reveals. What?" Melanie, with a frown.

"The man is serious." Lansana, taking up Garik's cause.

"More. Information." Melanie.

"I can get us to the storage room where it's kept. Stephen showed me." Garik considered his sudden need for access to the weapon. Repair? Destruction? He wasn't sure, but he had begun to breathe more rapidly with his need, drawing in more and more air. His heart, pumping more blood, preparing his body for any demand it might be called upon to meet. "If we can get inside."

"I am French toast, yes?" Lansana reached past Melanie and pushed on Garik's shoulder. The scarification around her eyes and up across her head seemed to glitter in the dim light. "The wall. That was me."

"And. I. Shared." Melanie.

"If you people are doing this, so are we." Anatoli and Andrey together.

"Challenge accepted." Jacqueline. "We must move now. Devon needs his key by nine."

Garik had a new pack. It seemed they had as much interest in assisting him as he did in protecting them. He grinned.

"Follow me."

ow did I not see this?" The sword, just on the other side of the wall, and Garik couldn't get to it.

"My shoulder," Lansana said, "did not see it, either."

"Bet you felt it," Anatoli joked. The wall—beyond which Garik had assured them they would find the electrified sword—bore multiple imprints of her shoulder but no breakthroughs.

"Let me think." Garik's innate sense of actionable

probabilities, his "prescience" ability, had become jumbled in the storm of his building excitement at gaining access to the sword. He pressed his hand to the wall. "This room wasn't on the original plans, so it must have been added later."

"With. Reinforcement." Melanie had run at Lansana repeatedly until she had claimed she could do no more.

"A vault," Anatoli offered.

"This, perhaps, is something?" Andrey knelt to a panel on the lower portion of the wall. He traced several words with a finger and read, "High voltage. Carriage drive access only. Last serviced—" and he read off several inked-in dates, the most recent one a year earlier. He flipped two catches along the top edge, and the panel lifted away. Inside were two breakers and a yellow and blue button, one labeled up and the other down, plus some other electronic components.

"Perhaps." Garik knelt beside Andrey and he stroked the yellow button. The future was sliding into place once more, his options forming before him, the path that was his *right now* branching out to *probabilities,* lesser *possibilities,* and finally a series of branching *options* that faded before him even as he reached for them. He glanced toward the ceiling. "The vault may be reinforced, but the path up and down, likely not. Here's what we're going to do."

He pushed the yellow button and cocked his head to listen to the lifting mechanism as it began to turn. A gear drive, the most dependable form of mechanical conveyance. He could hear the scissor-like arms pulling the ceiling of the vault aside and the glass case with the sword steadily rising. When he was satisfied, he pressed the button again, and the noise stopped.

"That. Helps. How?" Melanie.

"Yes, yes, I see." Jacquelien pressed her hand to the wall, looked toward the ceiling, and nodded. "This is reinforced. A floor up, access."

"If Stephen will help us." Garik pictured a door near the natatorium fronting a bump-out in a wide corridor. To the unschooled, it could be heating or cooling conduits. Now he placed it directly above the sword's vault. The shaft the sword traveled would need servicing occasionally. Stephen had access to the storage area, meaning he had a passkey that would open the door, that was if he could be trusted.

Tracking device. Why had he told Stephen that? Sometimes he was a fool even when he tried to be the best that he could be.

"CHILL, MY man. You're not the first to be tracked." Stephen, with his blond dreads, stood alongside Garik at the bump-out door, his passkey in his hand. The others lounged casually around them, a group of friends chatting, even if they were providing attentive cover for testing Stephen's key on the door.

"It didn't make me think nice things about you."

Stephen laughed aloud, to be shushed by Jacquelien's hand and looks from several of the others.

"That's funny?" The laugh pricked Garik's irritation.

"Lots of people don't think nice things about me."

"I expect they don't, not when you refuse to consider the feelings of others."

"Do you want me to insert this key or put it away until you quit insulting me?"

"I can't get past you blabbing to everyone."

"Just to the guys, and you can thank me. It makes you less Rodheimer's pet and more one of us."

"Pet? How's that? I don't get any special treatment from him."

"Jantzen's old suite at the top of the tower. Hmm, let's see, anything else? Yes. There's reinstatement into the program after breaking out *twice*. Plus praise every time he talks about you."

"And Sunchaser undermining every step I take." And my girlfriend being killed and my life stolen and all my friends gone, and that didn't touch the city being decimated because he was here. A real pet, yeah, a favorite of the guy in charge.

"Yeah, there's that, but the Director's the boss. He takes precedence over Sunchaser."

Lansana leaned in, "Still jawing? Thought we were doing something here. Tick tock. Devon needs his passkey back."

"Open it," Garik said.

Stephen's key, with his access to the storage and maintenance areas, worked, thunk, thunk, and he pulled the door back. It and the door opening were reinforced with metal plate. Light from behind Stephen and Garik fell into the opening.

It was the shaft they had expected to find, perhaps eight by eight in depth and width. Centering each wall, a well-lubricated gear track started below them and extended upward out of sight. And attached to it all, suspended in midair, a platform, the sword in its glass case in the middle, and room for two people to ride along on either side. It gleamed in the shadowed light, brighter than it ought, although the glass case was likely concentrating what light was available.

"The case. How do we access it?"

"That's the next challenge. Before, the Director has always done it. Lightning. Well, electricity, but it looks the same to me. We can create a committee to discuss it, but it wouldn't hurt to hurry."

Before they could decide on their next step, the overhead lights in the building dropped to half level, red emergency lighting spaced along the walls began to flash, and an alarm pulsed in a repeating pattern.

"Two minutes to lockdown," a voice intoned. "Move away from security doors and exit all elevators at the next floor. Remain where you are until you are okayed to return to your regular activities."

"I think they know we're here." Stephen stepped back and pushed the door to, sealing away the glass-encased sword. "We need to go."

"Where?" Garik asked.

"This way. We have to get upstairs." Stephen took off running northwest along the outside of the natatorium and away from the training area.

"How did I not see this?" Garik ran at Stephen's side, unclear on where they were headed. He was learning one thing: prescience was only as good as the information you could access. And today, he felt stupider than a rock.

EVERYONE CROWDED into a service elevator that ran from the storage area on Level 4 up to the research labs on Level 2. Without Stephen's passkey, it would have been impossible for them to gain access. Inside, another layer of required permission confronted them.

"Impending lockdown," the control panel said. "You will not have time to reach your destination. Override permission required."

The panel blinked for a hand scan, and Stephen placed his on the panel. It refused to scan and repeated, "Override permission required."

"Director Weston Rodheimer. Override permission granted."

"Thank you, Director Rodheimer. Have a good day."

The doors slipped shut with a ding, and the car began to move upwards one floor.

"Director Rodheimer?" Stephen looked behind him to see Anatoli grinning. "Which of you was Director Rodheimer?"

Andrey thumbed towards his brother, and Anatoli looked smug. He pumped a hand in the air. "Mocking-birds unite."

"So," Jacquelien said, "that's what he's good for. A chatterbox."

Anatoli struggled to reach her to pop her up beside the head, but his brother, Lansana, and Melanie managed to hold him back.

Garik laughed. He looked at the time displayed on the control panel. Fifteen of. They had time, and Devon wouldn't have to call security to get back into his apartment.

GARIK LAY in bed, his feet brushing the wall, and his head nearly touching on the opposite end. He now slept on his side or with his knees bent, a penalty for his extra DNA-driven height. He curled one arm around his pillow, and he worked his face into its softness. The scratch of hair on his cheek was new enough that it caught him off guard. He rolled to his back, looking at the ceiling.

He was partially pleased at his day.

Back by nine? Check, although Devon was already

inside. When the warning sounded, he was on his way to the apartment. At a security guard's approach, he rummaged in his pockets as though searching for his passkey, and the guard offered his, warning him to keep inside until the lockdown was over.

Find the final layer of schematics to the electrified sword? Check. They hadn't brought it with them. Garik already had it in his head, and no, he wouldn't forget. That's what the *photographic* in *photographic memory* meant, he had assured everyone present.

Locate the sword to prevent Sunchaser from using it to wreak havoc on anyone else's life? Partial check. They had located it but were unable to access it, not fully. It remained somewhere in limbo between the Level 4 vault and the research center's main lobby. Whether that was what had triggered the campus lockdown, no one had bothered to say, and Devon hadn't heard.

He finally drifted off to an old dream, a nightmare, really. A giant silverback gorilla chased him, and a man in black held out a sword that could defeat it, but only while Garik held the sword in the air. Self-doubt always made the sword sag in his hands, and each time, the gorilla wrapped its fist around Garik and began to squeeze, jarring him awake.

Garik now knew the characters in the nightmare. The gorilla was the Director, DNA bonded with the beast. The man in black was Jantzen Hefferly, but he was gone and could no longer help him. The sword still confused him. He'd never held it in his hands and had only seen it wielded twice. He couldn't even get to it to make the corrections he'd seen in the final page of the schematics, the one that Marisa had known was missing so long ago.

If he could do that . . . if he could do that . . . if he could do that . . . and he drifted off to face the silverback one more time.

THE NEXT morning revealed the scope of what Garik and his pseudo pack had accomplished. At first, Devon struggled with opening the door.

"Hey, kiddo. This thing's stuck, you come give it a try."

"Wimp," Garik teased. "Maybe it wants your palm-print." His head still spun with dreams of holding the sword aloft and letting it fall every time, and he wore a false sense of bravado for his "roomie."

"Not working."

"And mine should?" His passkey was good for the Tower to access Jantzen's apartment and not much else. He couldn't even move about the research center without piggybacking on Devon's.

The door opened as Garik approached it and revealed Airman Shan Vang standing alongside someone Garik didn't recognize.

"Mr. Shayk, I see you are still with us. Ah, Mr.

Maye. May I introduce Airman Collette Stephenson. Airman Stephenson will be assigned to you until the emergency is over."

"What emergency is that, Airman Vang?" Devon smiled.

"You are unaware?" Vang looked like he hardly believed it. "The sword has been stolen from its vault on Basement Level 4. Until it is recovered, no one can walk the premises without their assigned chaperone. Airman Stephenson will be ready to accompany you to breakfast when you are ready."

Stephenson greeted them. "Mr. Shayk, Mr. Maye," then turned her back to them and fell into parade rest, with her legs slightly apart and her hands behind her back.

Devon closed the door and turned to Garik. "You said you were looking for the final schematic, not to steal the sword."

"It was still there when I walked away. I swear." He held up his hand as a pledge of honesty, remembering the time he had pledged to behave with the same hand after having cut himself while breaking a mirror in frustration.

The sword. Stolen. Now he couldn't even repair or disable it. His last gift to Marisa, even that taken from him by the ineptitude of the Tower.

— 12 —

G

arik was back in Jantzen's apartment high in Corona Tower, banished by Weston Rodheimer.

He hadn't seen or spoken to Halo Sunchaser for the two weeks of his banishment, which was fine by him. His total link with humanity had been Kofi Mandela, meeting with him daily for physical training; and the delivery boy from the Stamford Suites Grill, Steve Tsuchiya, who rang his doorbell three times a day— whom Garik had learned almost nothing about, except that he was average height, had dark, very straight hair, and he wore the Corona Tower uniform very well. He was never creased and never stained.

Garik had also seen Dr. Jimenez every other day. Flexibility checks. Breathing capacity. The good doc had even ordered up a fancy treadmill so that he could run stress tests on his heart.

"You have all this equipment in the hospital. I ride the elevator very well. You can test me there." And get me out of this hamster cage, Garik thought. He could only look out the windows so many hours before he wanted to shake the dust of the Tower off his feet and be gone.

If there was any dust. He didn't know. Each day when he returned from his sessions with Kofi, his linens were freshened and the carpets vacuumed. And likely every item in the apartment searched for any contraband that Garik might have acquired THROUGH THE PLATE GLASS WINDOWS THAT DIDN'T OPEN.

Sheesh, this was getting old!

Dr. Jimenez had answered, "No, we can't," and he had refused to elaborate. Garik learned not to ask.

He had observed the portions of Bay City he could see from his windows, some towards the east but mostly south and west. The city had filled out with greenery. He could no longer see City View Apartments, his home for the first decade he'd lived in America. Bay City, once his home. It didn't feel much like home any longer.

Closer in, he'd spent hours watching the activity along Sycamore. From his height, the people along the sidewalks were very small, little more than ants. Several times he'd seen the ants moving very fast, skateboard fashion, and he'd remembered visiting the food court and Chow Down at the base of the Tower with his friends Ibn Hariri, Muhammad Saud, and Hayat al-Haber. It seemed a lifetime ago, even more, sometimes.

More unusually, in the first week, he had seen military transports making their way south from the Tower's base and down Sycamore. Most turned west at Ninth toward Argyle Station or possibly Interstate Transport; with others going north on Sycamore. The only reason for heading north was to access The Docks or Harbor Shipyards. After the first week, everything seemed to settle down.

He couldn't see the high school from his side of the building, but when he and Kofi were at the Stamford Suites pool, he tried to see if Colonel Brace's hybrid paramilitary troops were still stationed there. The glass wall along the pool was angled poorly to observe more than the roof, but he was no longer seeing young people on the streets during the day, and the white stylized eagle no longer flew from the school's flagpole.

His time with Kofi didn't even seem like training any longer, more like they were filling time until the next thing that happened.

Two weeks in was when it did.

DR. JIMENEZ reclined on Garik's couch—formerly Jantzen Hefferly's in a previous life—and observed Garik running on the treadmill. Garik wore shorts, socks and shoes, and leads with sticky pads attached to his chest and back.

"These are the same results we've seen the past two weeks. Is this all you have to give, Mr. Shayk?"

Garik continued to run, breathing evenly, not tired, and only perspiring enough to keep his body cooled to an optimal temperature. He thought, *No, Dr. Jimenez, it's not. You wouldn't believe your machines if I gave you all I've got to give.* Instead, he remembered what Jantzen once told him, to not give away everything he could do.

He also noted the doctor's use of his last name. Not once in the previous two weeks had he called him Garik, and in retaliation, Garik had called him nothing at all, refusing to use either his first name or his last, only resorting to Doctor when forced.

"It is time, then, to alter what we do. If you will clean up and change, I wish us to visit the research center. You may find a few differences. I will wait here." The man pulled out his tablet and tuned out Garik as though no longer in the same room with him.

Garik stopped the treadmill and began removing the

sticky pads. Not even Nurse Ratchett had been to visit him. The doctor had shown him how to attach the leads, and it had been Garik's responsibility each visit afterwards. He patted his face with a towel, left it draped over the treadmill, and headed for a shower.

He took his time under the water, letting it hit his back and shoulders until it burned. Why now? Why two weeks in? And why mention a few differences? How different could it be? People walking the corridors, the cafeterias serving up food, a few military types looking down on everyone else, and all the weird hybrid variations filling in the mix . . . life as normal in the Corona Tower basements.

Yet, on the way, it wasn't the same at all. Even with the Tower's super-purified air, the elevator smelled different. Unused. As if an element of humanity that couldn't be scrubbed from even the cleanest surface had been somehow removed.

Or maybe it was the lack of cleaning, the lack of the *necessity* of cleaning . . . an aroma missing . . . as much as he tried, Garik couldn't pinpoint it.

Reaching the hospital level, the sensation was stronger. The elevator doors opened to the ribbon-floored corridor that was Basement Level 4, with the blue stripes along each wall leading them forward.

Quiet. Everything so quiet.

"Where is everyone?" Garik knew it was the right question. He didn't hear . . . breathing, monitoring machines, footsteps, the rush of air as doors were opened and closed. His hearing was more acute than any human that had ever lived, and he realized he had adapted to the sounds of life as a backdrop that could be tuned out. Or better said, that he no longer had to tune out, but that he could hear selectively and pick up on individual sounds as he needed to hear them.

"So, you can tell?" The doctor paused and studied Garik for a moment. "Perhaps the Director is correct. There is the . . . slightest chance that you may be what he has been looking for all along." Then he shrugged. "It is not my call. Come. We have an appointment. Let's not keep them waiting. This way."

The doctor didn't motion, point, or pause. He simply moved forward, knowing Garik would follow.

GARIK WANTED to turn and walk out again when he saw the people waiting on him. Director Rodheimer across the room in a modern chair with thick arms. Halo Sunchaser behind him, her face hard. Colonel Brace, apart from them but still across the room from Garik. On the other side of the room, two bulky orderlies and Nurse Ratchett, all three prim and expressionless. In the center, a chair.

"For me, right?" It was the only option, and Garik lowered himself into it.

"So, my boy, the place to yourself." Rodheimer motioned around him. "Have you enjoyed it?"

"Enjoyed what? I've been in Jantzen's suite the entire time."

"Dr. Jamie?" Rodheimer looked at him and waited.

"I saw no need for him to move back and forth." The doctor shrugged.

"So be it. Now we are ready to move forward."

"And this is why you've emptied this facility, this boy?" Brace watched Garik with narrowed eyes.

"Hardly a boy, Colonel. He has evaded us in a full escape twice, and we are certain he was instrumental in stealing an artifact from the most secure vault in the most secure building in this city. All this and he left no trace of his presence."

"So you say." Brace didn't seem convinced.

"And he decimated your paramilitary on more than one occasion. You must give him that."

"I still do not understand why I am now responsible for all of your former experiments. You have room for them here."

"For two reasons, Colonel. The facility in Canada is now ready, and the Canadians wish it stocked with viable prospects for marketable skills. And as far as room, not for much longer. I am requesting three hundred of your men for volunteers. We can begin DNA sampling immediately."

Garik spoke up, "DNA sampling of what?"

"Of you."

"Like, cheek swabs?" Garik wasn't liking the sound

of this.

"Please inform him now, Dr. Jamie. I had asked to have these explanations cleared up before my return."

"I understand, Director. However, I have been testing him over the previous two weeks, and I am of the opinion he is far stronger than we originally estimated. If he wanted to escape . . . well, this is a very secure room. It was better to wait."

"Tell me *what*." Garik spat it as a demand, not a question.

"The harvesting method is a little more than a cheek swab, Mr. Shayk. We need spinal fluid to concentrate the DNA enough to bring about the required hybrid adaptations in the new volunteers."

"Feed them wolf juice like you did me."

"Yes, this I am still unclear about." Brace leaned forward, his expression doubtful. "You say the boy is intractable. Why do I want soldiers who will not follow orders?"

"Not intractable. Strong willed. That's what we are resolving. He was undisciplined when we got him. Your men have years of training. We will be starting with different stock, one that is already compliant, all provided the same DNA blend, just as we did with your paramilitary team."

"Only without flaws."

"Zero flaws. As you can see, he is perfect."

"And we can't just give my men the DNA mixture

you gave this boy? Surely they would turn out the same."

"Impossible. The DNA calibration is specific to each individual. The bonding has already happened with this one. No additional bonding required. Simply inject and wait for it to colonize the host body."

Brace fought a smile.

Garik tried to tamp down his breathing, settle his heart, but he didn't like this.

"How much spinal fluid?" He fought his voice as he said it, refusing to allow it to shake.

"All of it, my boy. That's why we can only move ahead with three hundred men at a time. We will take one from each group, and he will provide for the next three hundred."

"Not with me." Garik released the rainbows that hovered at the corners of his vision, but before they could fly, he felt something pierce his shoulder, and he slumped, the rainbows fading away.

"See, my boy, we know you better than you know yourself." The Director shook his head as if speaking to an imbecile. "Dr. Jamie, Nurse Leah, if you will direct your people to restrain the young man so he cannot escape this time. He's done that often enough. And you, Colonel, how soon can you provide your volunteers?"

"Three hundred, you say." He calculated. "Some will need to come overland. Three days. Will that do?"

"If this one doesn't escape before then." He walked

to Garik who was now on a gurney with his arms, legs, and head strapped to the table. "You, Mr. Shayk, have outdone yourself. And don't pretend you can't hear me. The drug affects your muscles, not your mind. I wondered for a time if the damage to our facilities and our reputation—yes, I worried about that—was worth it, or if you would fail me as the rest have. Jantzen nearly pulled you away, but Halo resolved that. But you, you were amazing! To break into our most secure facility! Impressive! We have yet to locate the sword, but I'm certain it will turn up, and if not, then I will have to ask Halo to build another one, so nothing lost and everything gained." Rodheimer turned, and in the turning dismissed Garik as a tiresome matter over and done with.

Garik shook with fury and then realized he wasn't shaking at all. The orderlies were rolling him out of the room, and he had no control over his actions.

Revenge. Revenge would be sweet . . . if Nurse Ratchett didn't suck him dry first.

In Book Ten, Garik Shayk, changed forever by his induction into the Human-Hybrid Project, takes on a new challenge.

The Russian's Revenge
Book Ten
The Human-Hybrid Project

Garik learns his trusted mentor, Jantzen Hefferly, is somehow still alive. He is compelled to effect a rescue, and then to bring the Tower's cruel leaders to justice. Garik faces one problem. Is he still human enough to manage the feat, or will his hybrid half destroy everything he once held dear?

The Human-Hybrid Project

Addictive!

A 10-book series you won't be able to forget. Explore each book, the characters, and more at our website www.thehumanhybridproject.com.

Book 1   Book 2

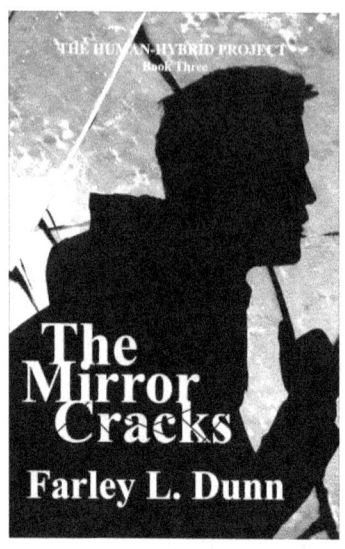

Book 3

Book 4

Book 5

Book 6

Book 7

Book 8

Book 9

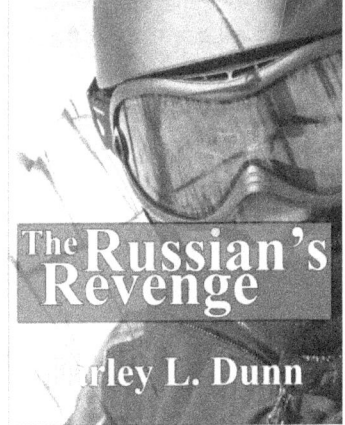

Book 10